The Golden Name Day

The Golden Name Day

by

JENNIE D. LINDQUIST

Pictures by

GARTH WILLIAMS

HARPER & ROW, PUBLISHERS

NEW YORK, EVANSTON, AND LONDON

CONTENTS

1. A Name Day   1
2. The Party   19
3. Yellow Roses   37
4. A Very Unusual Name   54
5. The Colored Window   76
6. The Apple Orchard   98
7. The Birch Gatherers   118
8. "The Funniest Club in the
      World"   145
9. Another New Friend   173
10. The Violet Basket   195
11. Plans and Secrets   213
12. The Golden Name Day   229

v

The Golden Name Day

Chapter 1

A NAME DAY

"PERHAPS it is a good thing after all that we didn't have this room papered last fall," said Grandma. "Nancy will enjoy picking out paper herself, and if she helps me put it on, it will seem more like her own room. And maybe it will help to keep her from being homesick."

"I'm sure it will," said Grandpa. "You have made the room look pretty anyway. Where do you want the bureau moved?"

"Just a little this way, toward the bed. I thought we'd put the little rocking chair here by the window. It will be a nice place for Nancy to sit when she wants to read, and later in the spring she can look out and see the lilacs coming into blossom."

Grandma looked around the room. "That's better," she said. "I will bring up my bowl of narcissus that is budding and put it on the window sill so that Nancy will have something to watch now. It will be good to have a child in the house again."

"Yes, it will," said Grandpa, "but I hope it won't be too hard on you. I hope we did right in saying we could take Nancy."

"Of course we did right," said Grandma. "This is where she should come. Don't worry about me. I kept waking up in the night thinking how hard it was going to be for her traveling all by herself this morning. This has happened so suddenly she must be pretty upset. After all, she's only nine. When you go to meet her, be sure you stand where she can see you as soon as she gets off the train."

Grandma leaned down and picked up the big cat who was rubbing against their ankles. "Poor little Nancy," she said, "once we get her here things will be all right. (Yes, yes, Teddy, you shall have your breakfast in a minute.) The animals will be a comfort to her."

"Yes, they will," said Grandpa, "and Sigrid

and Elsa and Helga, too." He smiled. "I expect they'll be up here most of the time now."

Grandma smiled too. "That will be good," she said, and they went downstairs together.

It was not only Teddy who was in a hurry for his breakfast. Oscar, Grandpa's dog, was hungry, too; and Karl the Twelfth was waiting impatiently for his oats and hay. Grandpa had given his animals unusual names. Karl the Twelfth and Oscar were named after famous kings of Sweden; and Teddy's real name was the same as that of the President of the United States, Theodore Roosevelt, whom Grandpa admired very much. Now he fed them all, petting each one as he did so, and making sure that everything was well with them. Then, after he and Grandma had had their breakfast, he harnessed Karl the Twelfth to the grocery wagon. It had been newly painted a dark red with white lettering:

E. A. BENSON   MEATS AND GROCERIES

"I'll stop at Anna's on my way to work now," he said to Grandma, "and I'll be sure to be at the station in good time for Nancy's train."

Sigrid and Elsa and Helga were just getting up when he opened the Carlsons' kitchen door. "Good morning, everybody!" he said.

"It's Grandpa!" cried Elsa and came running out of the bedroom with Sigrid and Helga following. "Oh, Grandpa, it's really the day. Nancy's coming today!"

"Are you going to meet her now, Grandpa?" asked Helga.

"Not now," he answered, trying to hug all three little girls at once. "She isn't coming until after eleven. I only stopped to do an errand for Grandma." He turned to their mother. "She wants to know if she may borrow your silver cake plate for this afternoon, Anna."

"Of course she may. I'll get it right off."

"I wish I could stay out of school and go to the station with you, Grandpa," said Elsa. "I really ought to go, because in two weeks I will be nine. In two weeks Nancy and I will be twins. I really ought to go to meet my twin."

"I'd like to have you all go," said Grandpa, "but school must come first. Nancy will be waiting for you this afternoon and Grandma says for you to come as soon as you can."

"We'll run," said Elsa, "but I wish we lived nearer you. I wish we lived right next door."

"It isn't so very far," said Grandpa, smiling at her. "It doesn't take you more than fifteen minutes to get there."

4

"Fifteen minutes is too far between friends," said Elsa decidedly.

"But you know the luckiest thing, Grandpa," said Sigrid. "We're getting out early today. It's teachers' meeting day and we get out at three and we'll be at your house by half-past. Oh, I can hardly wait!"

"We have three excited little girls today," said their mother, coming back with the cake plate. "You must tell Nancy how glad they are she is coming. Poor child, I'm afraid she's going to be pretty homesick; I don't believe she's ever been away from her mother and father before."

"But, Mamma," said Elsa, "you know what I was thinking? I was thinking that in stories when a little girl has to go away from home because her mother is sick, she always has to go somewhere where nobody wants a little girl at all. That's worse. Nancy is coming to a place where everybody wants her."

"I want her," said little Helga.

"We all want her," said Sigrid.

"I will tell her," said Grandpa, "and it is a good feeling to be wanted. And it is a good thing, too, that Grandma and I have you three to help us this year. We will all do our best to make Nancy happy."

Grandpa saw Nancy even before the train stopped. Her sad little face was pressed against the window. As soon as she got off the train, he picked her up and kissed her.

"Well, well, here's my girl," he said, "and here's Karl the Twelfth to meet you and Grandma waiting at home. She says to tell you she's glad you came today because she needs a little girl to help her. It's her name day and she's having a party."

He saw that Nancy was close to tears, but he pretended not to notice. He set her gently down on the ground, put his hand in his pocket and took out two pieces of sugar.

"I'll get your baggage," he said, "while you run give these to Karl the Twelfth. He's been asking and asking, 'When is Nancy coming? You grownups never give me enough treats.' "

Nancy smiled a little as she took the sugar. When she was very small, she had thought the animals really did talk to Grandpa because he so often told her what they said. Last summer Elsa had confessed that she had thought so, too. "In fact," she had added, "even now I don't think I'd be surprised if I came into the barn some day and found Grandpa and Karl the Twelfth and Oscar and Teddy, too, deep in conversation."

Elsa had read a great many library books and so was able to use interesting phrases like "deep in conversation," when most people would simply have said "talking."

Nancy fed Karl the Twelfth his sugar, and then stood with her cheek against his nose while she waited for Grandpa. He soon came back with her baggage, and they got into the wagon.

"Who's going to drive?" he asked.

Nancy brightened a little. "Oh, may I?" she said. Not that anybody needed to drive, really, for if there was one thing Karl the Twelfth knew better than anything else it was the way home at mealtime. Nancy would have had a hard time to make him go in any other direction, but she liked to hold the reins anyway.

"Grandma has been busy this morning," said Grandpa. "She has been baking her name day cake."

"What is a name day?" Nancy asked.

Grandpa looked at her in astonishment.

"Do you mean to tell me you have never been with us when we have been celebrating a name day?"

She shook her head. "I never have."

"It doesn't seem possible," said Grandpa, "but I suppose it must be that you never happened to come visiting us at any time when it was one of our name days." He smiled down at her. "Your mother was with our children so much when they were growing up that I forget you aren't a little Swedish girl. You seem to Grandma and me like our own little granddaughter. And to think we never told you about name days! But you know about our Swedish Almanac Book, don't you?"

"Yes, but I can't read it because it *is* Swedish," said Nancy.

"I guess you never looked at it closely. You'd be surprised to see how much of it you could read. You take a look at it again. There is a page for every month and opposite each date in the month is a person's name. Your name day comes on the date where your name is in the Almanac. On April twenty-second it's Albertina, and Albertina is Grandma's name; so today is her name day. That's why she's celebrating. Some of her friends will come to the party, and, of course, Sigrid and Elsa and Helga will come to play with you. You can't imagine how glad they are you're going to be with us."

"I'm glad they're coming this afternoon," said Nancy, "but what do you do on a name day?"

"First, the name day lady has to bake a cake."

"She has to bake it herself?"

"Yes. I don't know that they celebrate name days in the same way all over Sweden, but in the part where Grandma lived when she was a girl, it was the custom for the name day person to make a cake and invite her friends to a party. You'll know all about it before the afternoon is over. And you'll be with us when some of the children celebrate their name days at our house. That will be best of all."

"What do they do then?" asked Nancy.

"If it's in the spring or summer, they decorate the house with garlands of flowers. They wear their Swedish costumes and Grandma plays the piano so they can dance the Swedish dances. And the little girl who has the name day is the queen of the day. The other children make a little throne for her and a crown of flowers."

"A little queen with a crown of flowers!" said Nancy. "Oh my! Grandpa, when is my name day?"

Grandpa looked startled. "Well, now," he said, "I don't know if there is a Nancy Day. The Almanac has only Swedish names, you see."

"You mean maybe I don't *have* a name day?" asked Nancy, and she sounded so surprised and disappointed that he put his arm around her.

"Oh, I'm not sure, but I don't think Nancy is ever a Swedish name. I wouldn't worry about it, though. If you don't have a name day in the Almanac, Grandma'll be sure to think of some way to get one for you. You and she will have plenty of time to plan about name days and all sorts of things. Your Papa wrote me that you have been doing so well in school that you can have a vacation the rest of the term."

"Yes, I had a double promotion, so I skipped a grade." She moved closer to him and leaned against him. He looked down at her and saw how pale she was.

"It will do you good to be out-of-doors," he said. "You will get strong and rosy-cheeked. And Mamma will be getting stronger every day, too. You must try to remember that when it seems hard that she has to be away so long. It is a fine thing for her to go to a hospital where she can have such good care, but nothing will do her so much good as to know that you are happy."

"That's what Papa said, too." Nancy sighed. "But Mamma may be gone a whole year."

Grandpa evidently realized what a long time a year was, for he began to tell Nancy about things Grandma and the children were planning for her visit.

"And Aunt Martha has invited you to come out to the farm for a week soon," he went on, "when the apple orchards are in blossom, so you can see how pretty they are. I'll tell you something else. Grandma has been planning for some time to paper the spare room where you are going to sleep and now she is going to let you choose the paper so it will seem like your own little room. Would you like that?"

"Yes, I would, and I know exactly what kind of paper I'd like to have. I wanted it at home, but we had to have the kind the landlord put on. I'd like paper with little yellow roses on it. Grandpa, do you think I could have little yellow roses?"

"I don't see why not. Yellow roses seem to me a good thing to have on wallpaper."

"It would be like a storybook room," said Nancy. "It would be lovely. I will help Grandma put the paper on the wall; and I could cut off a little piece to send to show Mamma, couldn't I?"

"Indeed you could. You could even write her a little letter on the back of it."

Nancy sat quietly, thinking of the room with yellow roses. Grandpa was thinking, too, and presently he spoke his thoughts.

"Nancy, you have come at a beautiful time of year."

She looked up at him in surprise.

"Yes, I know," he said, "today is a gray day and we could hardly say whether it is April or November. But tomorrow or the next day the sun will begin to shine and everything in the earth will be growing. Soon a little green will show on the trees and you and the other children will find blue violets in the grass. Dandelions will be bright yellow on the lawns and the fruit trees will blossom. I have watched for many years, Nancy, and it is a wonderful thing to see—the earth changing from grayness into all the colors of springtime."

They were both silent again for a while and then Nancy smiled.

"Grandpa, what you said sounded like a poetry piece."

"Spring is like a poetry piece, Nancy. You have lived all your life in a big city and you don't know how wonderful spring can be. You wait, this year you'll see."

"I wish I could have a name day in the spring-time," Nancy said. "A person who had a name day then could have a little crown of violets or maybe of apple blossoms. Or maybe June would be better. The month of roses. A little name day queen with a crown of yellow roses! Oh my! Grandpa, do you have a name day?"

"Yes, mine comes on May 18, Erik Day."

"Do you have to make a cake?"

"No, Grandma has always made it for me, but do you know what I think? I think if you would help me, then I could make one. We'll have a try at it and if it doesn't turn out to be the best name day cake that ever was, I'll eat my hat!"

Nancy giggled. "This hat, Grandpa?"

"I should say not! Not this old one. My best straw hat with the silk band around it! So we'd better make a good cake, because I can't afford to buy hats to eat. But here we are, almost at home and just in time for dinner. And, Nancy, I have thought of something else. You are a lucky little girl. Most children have only one family, but hereafter you will always have two. You have Mamma and Papa, who think of you every day, and the time for you to go back to them will come faster than now seems possible. But this year we are your family—Grandma and I and Karl the Twelfth and Oscar and Teddy; and you are our little girl. Look! Here comes Oscar now and there is Grandma at the front door, holding Teddy."

17

Grandma had put on her best white Swedish apron in Nancy's honor; her white hair was combed smoothly back from her round, rosy face. She looked, Nancy always thought, like a grandmother in a storybook.

Nancy got down from the wagon and Oscar jumped up on her and almost knocked her over in his joy at seeing her again. She gave him one big hug and then gently pushed him aside. Grandma set Teddy down on the ground and Nancy ran into her arms.

"My, my," said Grandma, "it is good to have a little girl again."

Chapter 2

THE PARTY

At dinner Grandma wanted to hear all about Nancy's train ride and about her school and all the things she had been doing during the winter.

"And what about Charlotte?" she asked. "Didn't she come with you? I thought we'd make some new clothes for her. I have some pretty pieces you could use."

"Oh, yes, she came," said Nancy. "She's in the top tray of my trunk. Can I take her out right after dinner so she won't smother?"

"Yes," said Grandma. "We shan't have time to do all your unpacking before the party, but we'll certainly take out Charlotte and a dress for you to wear this afternoon."

They talked about name days, too, and Grandma understood how Nancy felt.

"Of course you want one. When the girls come this afternoon, you can all look through the Almanac. If there isn't a Nancy Day there, we'll have to think of some other way to find one for you. Every little girl ought to have a name day."

"Do you think a crown of yellow roses would be pretty, Grandma?"

"It would be lovely, and crowns of mixed flowers are pretty, too. Once when I was a little girl in Sweden, my mother's geraniums were blossoming so well on April twenty-second, that she let me pick enough leaves and red blossoms to make a crown. I thought it was beautiful. If you and I can't think of some way to get a name day for you, I'm sure somebody in the family will. So don't you worry. But now we'll have to get ready for the party this afternoon."

Grandpa and Karl the Twelfth went back to the grocery store, and Grandma and Nancy cleared the kitchen table and washed and dried the dishes.

Grandma had put her best white linen cloth on the dining room table, with one of her pink geraniums in the center. She was using her silver coffee service and her prettiest cups and saucers.

The children were going to have their party in the kitchen. "You may set your table any way you want to," said Grandma. Nancy went to the china closet to choose four of Grandma's little souvenir cups and saucers—almost as small as dolls' dishes. They would have their milk, flavored with a few drops of coffee, in these. She chose one cup with blue forget-me-nots on it, one with little pink rosebuds, one with tiny violets, and one with pink and blue flowers that neither she nor Grandma could name. There was no cup with yellow roses.

Grandma had made a small name day cake for the children, and she let Nancy select a geranium from the kitchen window sills for the center of the table. Nancy chose a bright red one, then decided it didn't match the cups and saucers. She tried a rosy pink Martha Washington geranium instead. That was better.

Next, she and Grandma went upstairs to unpack Charlotte and to get themselves ready. Nancy put on her pink-and-white-checked gingham dress; Charlotte wore her blue-sprigged muslin.

"You may be the doortender," said Grandma.

"You'll remember, won't you, to curtsy to each guest and make her feel welcome?"

"Yes, Grandma," said Nancy. "May I look at the Almanac Book while I am waiting?"

"If there is time," answered Grandma, but at that moment the doorbell rang; the party had begun. Nancy ran to open the door. There stood two of Grandma's friends. Nancy curtsied but she didn't have a chance to tell them or any of the other ladies who came that they were welcome. Before she could say a word they began to tell her how glad they were to see her and how nice it was that she was to be with Grandma. It was they who made her feel welcome! Each lady who came shook hands with Grandma and said something in Swedish.

"What do they say?" Nancy whispered, and Grandma answered, "I congratulate you on Albertina Day." Every lady said it; it seemed to be the proper thing to do on a name day. And everybody talked and laughed and acted as if name days, even for grownups, must be a great deal of fun.

The last person to come was Aunt Anna. Nancy completely forgot to curtsy; instead she threw her arms around her and hugged her tight.

"Now I'm going to have four little girls for a

while," Aunt Anna said, "and that suits me fine. My, the girls are excited to think you are here. How they will keep their minds on their lessons this afternoon, I'm sure I don't know. They'll be here right after school; they have to stop at home only a minute to get a package."

Most of the ladies had brought their handwork, and Nancy was kept busy threading needles and holding skeins of yarn, but all the time she was wishing Sigrid and Elsa and Helga would come. At three o'clock Aunt Anna said, "If I were you, I'd put on my hat and coat and go outdoors. I'm sure Oscar will want to play throw-the-stick until the girls come. We'll be having our coffee in a few minutes, but you'll want to wait for them."

Oscar was indeed glad to have Nancy throw his stick, and they played until they heard the girls coming. They were laughing, as usual, and were carrying a huge, awkward package wrapped in newspapers. Oscar ran to meet them, but Nancy, suddenly a little shy, stood still, waiting. Elsa was the first to see her.

"There's Nancy," she cried, "there's Nancy!" The little girls set the package down on the sidewalk and came running toward her. They threw their arms around her and hugged her; they danced around her in excitement. She had never imagined that they would be so glad to see her, and their pleasure gave her such a surprised, warm feeling that she couldn't think of a thing to say, but it didn't seem to matter.

"Come on, everybody," said Sigrid, "let's get the package and go in the house. Oh, Nancy, we'll have fun while you're here!"

All four little girls now helped to carry the package, and Oscar tried to help, too, but he just kept getting in the way. They were still laughing when they reached the kitchen. Grandma excused herself from the coffee table and came to greet them.

"What *is* all this, darlings?" she asked. "What in the world have you got in that package?"

"It's for you, Grandma," said Helga. "We raised it for you all ourselves. I helped, too. I watered it most every day." "A lady gave it to us when it was tiny," said Sigrid, "and we raised it for you. It took ages." "And once," said Elsa, "you came when we didn't know you were coming and we had to run like anything to hide it. Open it, please, Grandma."

Grandma opened the package and there was one of the most beautiful plants Nancy had ever seen. It had fresh green leaves and white blossoms—so many of them that they covered the

plant and spilled over the sides of the pot, making a little vine. All the ladies got up from the coffee table and came to see the present.

"But, dear children," said Grandma, "how did you ever grow such a lovely star-of-Bethlehem? I have never seen such a beautiful one."

The little girls' faces shone with joy, and it was easy to see that Grandma thought she had the most wonderful granddaughters in the world.

"Mamma helped a little," said Sigrid, "and Papa helped me paint the pot white so it would look pretty."

"We must put it on the parlor table," said Grandma. "I don't know how to thank you."

"There's a joke about it," said Elsa. "The lady that gave it to us said that star-of-Bethlehem plants blossom in September, never in spring. But this one didn't blossom in September at all; it waited for your name day!"

"Then it is even more wonderful than I realized at first," said Grandma.

Aunt Anna looked at the little girls. "You forgot something," she whispered. They understood what she meant and now each one curtsied and said in Swedish, "I congratulate you on Albertina Day."

"Name days seem to be a lot of fun," said

Nancy when the ladies had gone back to their party and the children had settled down in the kitchen.

"If you think this is fun," said Elsa, "you just wait until one of us children has a name day. That's more fun than *anything*!"

"Grandpa told me about it on the way home," said Nancy. "It must be wonderful."

"Nancy," said Elsa suddenly, "when's your name day?"

"I don't know if I have one," said Nancy.

"Everybody has a name day," said Helga.

"No, they don't," said Sigrid, "not if they're not Swedish. Some of the girls in my room didn't know about name days. Mamma says they're not an American custom. Is your name in the Almanac, Nancy?"

"Grandma said you'd help me look."

"We will," said Elsa and ran for the Almanac. "We can eat our cookies and look at the same time and have our cake afterward. Come on, let's hurry; I can't wait to see if Nancy has a name day."

They crowded around the book. First, Sigrid showed Nancy the page for April so that she could see Albertina Day. Then they went back to January and looked carefully through every

APRIL.

Dagar.			☉ Upp.	Ned.		☽ Ned.	
1	T	Harald	5.44	6.24	♌	4.24	
2	F	Gudmund	5.42	6.25	♌	4.52	☿ u. 5.15 f. m.
3	L	Ferdinand	5.41	6.26	♍	5.16	☺ Fj.

Herrens nattvard, 1 Kor. 11.
Luk. 22: 14—22.

4	S	**Palm-Söndag**	5.39	6.27	♍	5.39	Ambrosius
5	M	Nanna	5.37	6.29	♍	Upp	○ 2.26 e. m. ☋
6	T	Vilhelm	5.36	6.30	♎	7.22	♀ u. 5.30 f. m.
7	O	Ingemund	5.34	6.31	♎	8.23	♂ u. 2.19 f. m.
8	T	Hemming	5.32	6.32	♎	9.26	
9	F	**Lång-Fredag**	5.31	6.33	♏	10.30	Otto
10	L	Ingvar	5.29	6.34	♏	11.38	♃ n. 4.3 f. m

Kristi uppståndelse, Mark. 16.
Matt. 28: 1—8. Ef. 1: 16—23.

11	S	**Påsk-Dag**	5.27	6.35	♐	f. m.	Ulf
12	M	**2 Dag Påsk**	5.26	6.36	♐	0.36	♄ u 5.18 f. m. Julius
13	T	Artur	5.24	6.37	♐	1.32	☾ 8.28 f. m.
14	O	Tiburtius	5.23	6.38	♑	2.22	
15	T	Olivia	5.21	6.39	♑	3.04	
16	F	Patrik	5.20	6.40	♒	3.41	
17	L	Elias	5.18	6.41	♒	4.13	☿ u. 5.15 f. m.

Jesus går genom lyckta dörrar, Joh. 20.
Luk. 24: 36—48. Ap. G. 13: 26—41.

18	S	**1 e. Påsk**	5.16	6.43	♓	4.43	☊ ☺ N. Valdemar
19	M	Olaus Petri	5.15	6.44	♓	Ned	● 10.49 e. m.
20	T	Amalia	5.13	6.45	♈	7.40	♀ u. 5.12 f. m.
21	O	Anshelm	5.12	6.46	♉	8.57	
22	T	Albertina	5.10	6.47	♉	10.10	♂ u. 1.54 f. m.
23	F	Georg	5.09	6.48	♉	11.19	
24	L	Vega	5.08	6.49	♊	f. m.	

Den gode herden, Joh. 10.
Joh. 10: 1—10. Hebr. 13: 20—21.

25	S	**2 e. Påsk**	5.06	6.50	♊	0.20	Markus
26	M	Engelbrekt	5.05	6.51	♋	1.11	♃ n. 3.2 f. m.]
27	T	Teresia	5.03	6.52	♋	1.52	☽ 2.34 f. m.
28	O	Ture	5.02	6.53	♌	2.27	♄ u. 4.19 f. m.
29	T	Tyko	5.00	6.54	♌	2.56	
30	F	Mariana	4.59	6.55	♌	3.21	☺ Fj.

month. They found one name after another that they knew. They looked and looked. They came to the thirty-first of December. In all the Almanac there was no Nancy!

"Mamma, Mamma," cried little Helga, running right in to the coffee party, "Nancy hasn't got any name day!" The other girls followed her. Ordinarily, they would have been told that they must not interrupt the grownups, but now everybody seemed to understand what a serious situation this was.

"That's because Nancy isn't a Swedish name, darling," said Aunt Anna.

"But, Mamma," said Elsa, "then she can't have any name day party. Oh, Mamma, isn't there an American Almanac?"

"Not one with name days in it, I'm afraid. You are lucky little girls, you know, because Grandma and Grandpa see to it that you have all the Swedish celebrations and holidays as well as the American ones. But we'll have to do something about a name day for Nancy. Of course she wants one. We'll think of something. It would be too bad if all of us put together couldn't think of some way to get a name day for her."

"Don't you worry, children," said Grandma. "You run back and have your cake now. Every-

30

thing will come out all right. And remember, Nancy, Grandpa said you were going to help him make his name day cake. Skip along now."

Helga was impressed. "You're going to help Grandpa make a cake?" she asked as they went back to the kitchen.

"Yes, and Grandpa said that if it wasn't the very best name day cake that ever was, he'd eat his straw hat with the silk band around it."

"I guess you'll make a good cake," said Elsa, "but I almost wish you wouldn't. I'd like to see Grandpa sitting right in that rocking chair chewing away at his best hat!"

"But it might make him sick," said Sigrid.

"Oh, dear," said Elsa, "you'd better make a mighty good cake, Nancy. And we'll all be thinking of a way to get a name day for *you*, too. You just have to have one."

There was so much to talk about and so many plans to make that the rest of the afternoon flew by; and all too soon it was time for the Carlson girls to go home.

Nancy had had such a good time that she was completely surprised herself when at the supper table she suddenly felt that she couldn't get along without Papa and Mamma another minute; and, before she knew what she was doing, she had put her head down on the table and begun to cry.

Grandma did not seem surprised at all. She got up, went over to Nancy, lifted her gently and led her to the rocking chair. She sat down and took Nancy in her lap.

"Oh, Grandma," Nancy sobbed, "I didn't mean to cry on your name day. I didn't mean to."

"Of course you didn't, Little One. But a good cry never hurt anybody. You have had a long, exciting day and you're all tired out. We'll go right up and get you ready for bed, and when you're all tucked in, Grandpa will come and sing you to sleep. And in the morning things will look much better."

Nancy couldn't believe things would ever look better, but she went with Grandma and was soon tucked in under the gay patchwork quilt. Then Grandpa came and sat beside her bed. There was a light in the hall, so she could see him dimly. She could feel his comforting big hand on hers.

Softly he began to sing little Swedish folk songs that all his children and grandchildren loved. Whenever they were sick or in trouble, as Nancy was now, Grandpa came and sang to them, and all their lives they would remember the good, safe feeling that stole over them as he sang.

"Please sing *'Tryggare Kan Ingen Vara,'* Grandpa," said Nancy. It was the song they all loved most at times like this—even before they could understand the words. Nancy couldn't understand them all now, but she knew what the song was about. Grandpa had told her. It was about God's little children and how safe they were in His hands, safer even than the stars in the heavens, safer even than the little birds in their cozy nests . . .

Grandpa sang until Nancy was fast asleep. Then he and Grandma sat for a long while in the kitchen talking about things they could do to make this hard year a happy one for her.

But Nancy slept. She did not hear them come up the stairs or even know that Grandma came to be sure she was still tucked in. She slept and slept —until suddenly a thump on her bed startled her wide awake. For a minute Nancy did not know where she was. Then she realized that the thump had been made by Teddy, come to tell her it was time to get up. She was at Grandma's. It was a lovely day. Today she and Grandma would pick out wallpaper. The Carlson girls would come often to play. There would be a week at Aunt Martha's. And it would be too bad if all of them put together couldn't find a name day for her.

She looked around the room. The sun came pouring in through Grandma's clean, clean windows and the crisp white curtains. It shone on the patchwork quilt and on Nancy's brown pigtails. It shone on Teddy's broad tiger-striped back and, when he turned toward the window, on his snowy-white shirt front. It shone on Charlotte sitting in the little rocking chair Grandma had painted a soft gray-green and on the table where the girls had left two library books for Nancy to read. It shone on the rather faded walls that soon would be shining back, gay with little yellow roses.

Nancy gave Teddy a loving squeeze and hopped out of bed.

Chapter 3

YELLOW ROSES

"Good morning, Nancy!" Grandma called. "I thought if I let Teddy go up he'd wake you. Put on your slippers and bathrobe and come downstairs. There's somebody here to see you."

Who could it be? Nancy hurried downstairs, Teddy dashing on ahead of her. It was Aunt Martha. She had driven in from the country to bring eggs for Grandpa's store. It was only half-past eight but here she was, with her errand all done, ready to join Grandma in a cup of coffee. Grandpa and Karl the Twelfth had long since gone to work.

Nancy was delighted to see Aunt Martha. Children could always be sure that there would be something exciting going on when she was around. She was not married but she knew how to play with children just as well as if she had had a dozen of her own. She kept house for Grandpa's older brother, Uncle Sven, and helped him take care of his farm and all his animals. Grandma said that Martha was the only one of their children who had inherited Grandpa's way with animals; they talked to her, too. Now she began to tell Nancy what Danny, the big farm dog, had said.

"Danny tells me that when he was way out in the pasture yesterday he found some mayflowers about ready to blossom and he thinks that you and Sigrid and Elsa and Helga had better come out tomorrow to see them. Uncle Sven is coming into town in the morning and he will call for you about eleven o'clock, and then we can all drive back to town in time for church Sunday morning."

Nancy was thrilled. "We can stay *overnight*?"

"Grandma says you may if you will take a nap this afternoon and rest tomorrow morning before Uncle Sven comes for you. You mustn't get too tired."

"I got you up this morning," said Grandma,

"because Martha says she will give us a ride down-street to pick out wallpaper if we can be ready soon after nine. And you must eat a good break-fast first. We will stop on the way home to ask Aunt Anna if the girls may go tomorrow. And I will tell you a secret. I have decided that you may give my *efter-kalas* out at the farm this time. We will pack the things in a box and get Uncle Sven to hide it in the wagon so the other girls won't see it; and you can surprise them when you come back from mayflowering. Won't that be fun?"

"Oh, yes!" said Nancy. This was the way things always were at Grandma's—something in-teresting happening every minute. She went to wash her face and hands and then came back to eat her breakfast. Grandma and Aunt Martha were talking to each other in Swedish. Nancy couldn't understand what they were saying, but she didn't mind; she was busy with her own thoughts.

An *efter-kalas*! Nancy knew what that word meant. An *efter-kalas* was an "after-party"; and it was a Swedish custom just as name day celebrating was. When a Swedish lady got ready to give a party, she was always so afraid that she might not have refreshments enough to go around for everybody that she prepared far too many. There were always a great many good things left over. These could not be wasted, nor could they be eaten for ordinary meals. Instead, the lady gave an "after-party," with the leftovers for refreshments. If, for instance, the first party had been for her relatives only, or for the ladies of her church, the "after-party" might be for some of her neighbors who didn't come to the first party. Sometimes Grandma, instead of giving her own *efter-kalas*, let one of the children give it; and that was what she was going to let Nancy do now.

There were plenty of cookies left, Nancy knew, and some Swedish coffee bread. The name day cake was all gone but that didn't matter. You wouldn't want to be eating name day cake on the wrong day. There would have to be something to drink, of course. Most ladies would serve children milk, or maybe lemonade—but not Aunt Martha. She would give them something they had never thought of. They could put their may-flowers on the table to make it look pretty. They would see the animals and go out in the woods; and then all the children would sleep together in the big open attic.

"What are you smiling at?" asked Aunt Martha, but she didn't wait for an answer. "Finish your oatmeal and get dressed or you won't be ready in time."

Nancy hurried with her last few spoonfuls and ran up to her room. Grandma helped with her pigtails, and then they all went out to the barn. Aunt Martha had driven into town in the buggy; and Whoa-Emma, the horse, was waiting, as eager for sugar as Karl the Twelfth always was.

Whoa-Emma was the same chestnut-brown color as Karl the Twelfth and they both liked sugar; otherwise they were as different as two horses could be. Karl the Twelfth was slow and steady and comfortable. Whoa-Emma took notions. One never knew what she would do.

She was pretty sure to be all right in the city, but on a country road, Grandpa and Uncle Sven said, you'd think she was a race horse. She might be walking along slowly and sedately when, all of a sudden, off she'd go like a streak! "Whoa, Emma! Whoa, Emma!" Uncle Sven or Aunt Martha would cry. But would Emma "whoa"? She would not—not until she felt like it. It was exciting and Nancy loved it, although she always felt a little frightened. You had to hang onto your hat and the side of the wagon, too, when Whoa-Emma was off like a streak.

Nancy went on thinking about her as they

drove downstreet. What if she should streak right by the wallpaper store! To be sure, she never had taken a notion to be off like the wind in the city, but who knew when she might? No, it was all right this time. Here they were at the store and Whoa-Emma was willing to stop. Aunt Martha hitched her, and the two ladies and Nancy went in to look at paper.

Aunt Martha told the clerk what they wanted and he brought out a roll of paper; it had yellow roses on it, but they were much too big. Grandma and Aunt Martha could see that they were, too.

"Small yellow roses for a little girl's bedroom," said Aunt Martha. The clerk tried again. He showed them another roll—it was a heavy paper, not exactly what Nancy wanted but it did have little yellow roses.

"I am afraid that is too expensive," said Grandma. "We can't pay more than six cents a roll."

Nancy had never thought of that—that the paper might be too expensive. She began to be really worried.

"Does it have to be *yellow* roses?" asked the clerk. "I think I have what you want in pink." He took down another roll; it was right except for the color. He and Grandma and Aunt Martha all

looked at Nancy. She did not have to say anything.

"H-m-m," said the clerk, "I can see that yellow roses are very important. I will see if we have anything down in the storeroom."

He went downstairs. At last he came back smiling. He must have found some yellow roses. If only they were the right kind!

He unrolled the paper; it was like that with the pink roses, but these roses were yellow, the yellow of gold and of sunlight, the yellow that makes this kind of rose the most beautiful flower in the world. The paper was exactly right. And it cost only five cents a roll! The grownups looked almost as happy as Nancy.

The clerk wrapped enough rolls of paper for one small bedroom. Grandma, Aunt Martha, and Nancy thanked him for all his trouble and went out of the store. Whoa-Emma had taken a notion to pull herself forward enough to enjoy a little lunch of a few twigs from a young maple tree by the sidewalk.

"Good gracious, Whoa-Emma!" cried Aunt Martha. "What will you think of next? Come back here! The trees on this street belong to the city. You'll be getting us arrested and what will Uncle Sven say if he finds we have all gone to jail.

Besides, horses shouldn't eat trees anyway and you had a good lunch at Grandma's. Come back here! Shame on you!"

Whoa-Emma, with a maple twig still sticking out of her mouth, let Aunt Martha pull her away. Nancy and Grandma looked anxiously up into the tree.

"She can't have been at it long," said Grandma. "I guess she hasn't done any harm, but you'll have to be careful where you hitch her next time, Martha."

"You always have to be careful with Whoa-Emma," sighed Aunt Martha. "The trouble is she'll do something else next time that nobody but her would ever think of. It never occurred to me that she'd try to eat a tree when the leaves aren't even out on it."

They got into the buggy and drove to Aunt Anna's, Nancy holding the wallpaper package because she could not bear to put it down.

Aunt Anna was glad to see them all and insisted that the ladies should have a cup of eleven-o'clock coffee before they left. It was all ready on the stove. "Of course the girls may go to the farm," she said. "They'll be so happy. And, Nancy, I have an idea about a name day for you."

Nancy looked up eagerly.

"I never saw you girls together long," said Aunt Anna, "before you were beginning to play you were somebody else. I was wondering who you were all going to be this summer."

Nancy understood what she meant—it was always fun to pretend they were storybook children and to call each other storybook names—but what did that have to do with a name day?

Aunt Anna went on, "Why don't you choose some name from the Almanac and pretend you are a little girl who has come over from Sweden to visit Grandma? The girls think it is a fine idea; they will call you that name and I will make a little Swedish costume for you. And we'll all plan the nicest name day party ever."

Nancy could hardly speak; she wanted to cry. Aunt Anna and the girls, who usually understood so well, hadn't understood at all this time. "It wouldn't be my real name," she said in a small voice. She didn't want to look at Aunt Anna or Grandma or Aunt Martha. They were all silent for a minute; then Aunt Anna drew Nancy toward her.

"I can see that wasn't a good idea," she said. "We should have known better. Of course only your very own name would do, and this is one time when pretend won't work. Don't you worry. We'll try again. We'll think of *something*."

"Will the girls care if I don't pretend it?" asked Nancy, still troubled.

"Of course they won't. They'll understand. Now tell me, did you get the wallpaper?"

"Yes, we did," said Nancy, "and it's exactly right." She unwrapped the package and showed it to Aunt Anna.

"We'll begin papering first thing next week," said Grandma.

"Grandpa said I could write a little letter to Mamma on the back of a piece of the paper," said Nancy.

"That's a good idea," said Aunt Anna, "and I can tell you something else you could do. The girls are already thinking about making May baskets. I know how you could make a little folding May basket that would go right into an envelope. You could write your letter on the inside of the basket and then Mamma could have it either flat like a letter or folded to stand up like a basket."

"What a good idea!" said Aunt Martha. "The flowers would be on the outside of the basket instead of inside as they usually are. When Mamma had read the letter, she could set the

48

basket on the table by her bed and keep little things like pins in it."

Nancy thought it was a wonderful idea. "Can we make it soon?" she asked.

"Yes, we can. If Grandma will let you, you can stay to dinner with the girls and then take a rest while they are in school this afternoon. They'll be home soon after half-past three and we'll have time to make the basket then. About five o'clock they'll walk home with you."

"May I, please, Grandma?" asked Nancy, and her eyes were shining.

"Yes, I think that will be nice," said Grandma, and they all smiled at Nancy, glad to see that she was happy again. "But now, Martha, we'd better be going or Grandpa won't have any dinner. You cut off a small piece of the paper for your basket, Nancy, and we'll take the rest home."

As soon as they had gone, Aunt Anna and Nancy set the table for dinner, and before long Sigrid and Elsa and Helga came running and skipping up the street. They were surprised and happy to see Nancy and to hear about the May basket. They understood about the name day.

"I see what you mean, Nancy," said Sigrid. "I guess I wouldn't want a pretend name for a name day either. We'll have to think some more. We'll get you a name day somehow even if we have to write a new Almanac!"

Nancy giggled. She knew they couldn't do that, but surely they would think of something. She took a nap after the girls had gone back to school and as soon as they came home again they began on the basket.

Aunt Anna sat down with them at the kitchen table and showed how to do it. "We will make a pattern first," she said, "out of old scrap paper so that we won't spoil any of the pretty wallpaper. First we'll measure and cut out a square nine inches on each side. Then we'll draw a pattern on it."

Step by step she showed the little girls what to do.

"Now the pattern is ready to cut," she said. "But be careful to cut only on the solid lines. Then fold your pattern on the dotted lines. Then put the tabs through the slits opposite them. Usually we'd have shorter tabs, because the basket would be fastened together with paste if we were not going to fold it and put it in an envelope. Good long tabs like this will hold it together even without paste, though, and then Nancy's Mamma can put the basket out flat and read the letter as often as she wants to."

This is one-half the size of Nancy's basket.

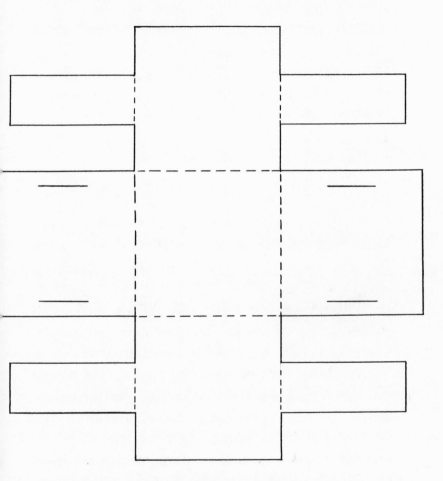

Cut on solid lines; fold on dotted lines.

Nancy followed Aunt Anna's directions carefully and, sure enough, the pattern made a little basket! After that, it was easy to trace the pattern on a piece of the wallpaper.

"Wait a minute before you cut the wallpaper, Nancy," said Elsa. "Mamma, couldn't she make scallops around the top edge of the basket? It would look fancier."

"A good idea," said Aunt Anna.

"I've got a penny for her to trace," said Helga. "I'll get it."

"I think a penny would make the scallops too big, dear," said Aunt Anna. "Please get me my pocketbook instead, and I will see if there is a dime in it."

A dime was the right size. All the little girls knew how to make scallops this way. Nancy put a mark on each edge of the dime, about halfway down. Then she put the top even with the top of the basket and traced half-circles, one after another. Then she cut the basket carefully. The scalloped edges made it look unusual.

"Couldn't you cut out a rose and paste it on the bottom?" said Sigrid. "You know the way cups sometimes have flowers at the bottom. That would make it fancier still."

They all agreed that it would; so Nancy cut

and pasted the rose. Then she folded the basket and fastened it together with the tabs. It was a lovely May basket.

"If you were going to give it to someone here," said Aunt Anna, "we could cut a handle and paste it on, but then Mamma couldn't open it to read her letter."

"We can make some of our May baskets this way and have handles," said Elsa, "and Nancy can make some more."

"So you can, but now I think Nancy'll have to go home. I promised Grandma, you know."

"But she hasn't written the letter," said Helga.

"It will be easier for her to do that when she is alone," said Aunt Anna. "I'll wrap the basket carefully so that it won't get torn or dirty, and then you'd better run along. You'll come right back, won't you, girls? You'll see Nancy tomorrow, you know. Just stop long enough to say hello to Grandma."

"And Oscar and Teddy?" asked Helga.

"Oh, of course," answered Aunt Anna, laughing.

And off they went.

Chapter 4

A VERY UNUSUAL NAME

THE next morning Nancy woke early and, taking a stick that lay on the chair beside her bed, pounded on the floor. This was a signal she and Grandma had thought of. Because Nancy was supposed to rest a great deal, she was to be allowed to sleep as late as she wished, and when she did wake up, she could pound on the floor. Then Grandma would open the hall door and let Teddy come upstairs to greet her. Nancy loved to have him in bed with her for a few minutes in the morning, and now that she was here he was to have a treat each day when she had breakfast. Teddy, brought up in a good Swedish-

American household, drank coffee. He not only drank it; he demanded it. Every morning before Grandpa had breakfast he prepared a saucer of coffee (one-third coffee, two-thirds cream and sugar) for his small friend. Teddy gave Grandpa no peace until the saucer of coffee was on the floor.

Nancy thought the idea of a cat drinking coffee was so funny that she was to be allowed to give him a second saucerful each day. "What if he isn't around when I have breakfast?" she had asked. "Don't you worry," Grandma had answered. "Teddy is a smart cat. It won't be long before he gets onto the new program; he'll be there all right. He and I, we'll have some coffee when you have breakfast, and then you and I can have a good chat. It will be our visiting time."

So Nancy pounded with her stick and listened. She heard Grandma's step, then the hall door open, and up came Teddy and leaped onto her bed.

"Hi, Teddy," she said, "we've got to get up this morning. No being lazy. Where's Oscar? I suppose he's out visiting all the neighbors as usual."

For that was Oscar's morning program. Oscar was a great caller. He was the only dog in the near neighborhood, and every morning he felt that he had to go to each neighbor's house to see that everything was all right. Often he was invited in and nothing pleased him more, for "Sociability," Aunt Martha used to say, "is Oscar's middle name." He could never have taken Danny's place as a watchdog at the farm. "Nancy," Grandpa once said, "if you ever hear any noises downstairs in the night, don't be afraid. It will probably be burglars that Oscar has invited in to have coffee."

Nancy could picture Oscar up on his hind legs, with one of Grandma's aprons tied around his middle, happily serving coffee to a couple of astonished burglars. All the animals—the ones at Grandpa's and those at Uncle Sven and Aunt Martha's—were a great joy to her, for she had no pets of her own. Every one of these animals was different from the others; each had his own ways and funny tricks and habits. "Grandpa's and Aunt Martha's animals have souls," said Elsa, and Nancy agreed with her. She never tired of watching them and playing with them. She looked at Teddy now and patted him gently, the funny, coffee-drinking cat.

"Come on, Ted," she said. "Let's go downstairs so I can give you your treat."

Grandma had Nancy's breakfast ready and helped her to prepare Teddy's coffee.

"Look, Grandma, I think Teddy knows we're getting something ready for him."

"Of course he does. I told you he was a smart cat."

It was easy to see that Teddy approved of the new custom. Nancy watched him eagerly lapping the coffee and then, before she sat down for her own breakfast, she opened the piazza door and looked out at the morning.

"It's a lovely day, Grandma," she said, sniffing the air. "It smells like spring; it smells like spring and summer all mixed up together."

"Yes, it's very warm for this time of year," said Grandma. "You'll have a good day in the country."

"Shall I pack my suitcase with my Sunday clothes?"

"No, you'll just need to take your nightgown and slippers. Aunt Martha will bring you back early enough in the morning so that you can get dressed for church here. We don't want to load Whoa-Emma too much or give Martha too much work. Now come have your breakfast, and then after you are dressed and all ready, why don't you write your letter to Mamma and go out and mail it and then come back and read your library books until Uncle Sven comes?"

So that was Nancy's morning program.

The afternoon at Aunt Martha's was even lovelier than the little girls had expected it would be. It took about an hour to drive to the farm so it was noon when they turned in at the road that led to the farmhouse. Danny came running to meet them; Cicily-Ann Sinkspout was sitting on the porch in the sun; there were several other cats near the barn; the hens could be heard making their funny little noises down in the henyard. Oh, it was good to be there!

Aunt Martha came to the door. "Hello, chickens! Hurry up and come have dinner; we want to get out into the woods while the sun is high."

The little girls clambered out of the wagon and helped Uncle Sven carry in the groceries he had bought in town. The Carlson children had not been at the farm for several weeks, and Nancy had not been there for nearly a year. There was so much to see and do that they didn't know where to begin.

"Begin with dinner," said Aunt Martha.

It was a merry meal, and as soon as it was over

she asked, "How many little girls vote to leave the dishes and go out in the woods right off?" Every hand went up. "How many will help do dishes when we come home?" Every hand went up again.

The children were delighted. The other grownups in the family would not have suggested such a plan. Dishes first, fun afterward, was their rule; but rules like that never bothered Aunt Martha.

"The dishes will wait; the sun won't," she said. "I'll put the food away and then we'll go. Run call Danny."

It was wonderful to be out in the woods. Danny and the children danced and ran about as if spring had got into their bones, and Aunt Martha, who loved to be out-of-doors, was as gay as they were. It was Helga, skipping ahead with Danny, who found the first delicate pink mayflowers peeking up through the old dead leaves. All the others came running to see and to smell. The little girls got down on their knees and stuck their noses right into the earth.

"They have the most beautiful smell of any flower in the world," said Sigrid. "Aunt Martha, why do you suppose they smell so lovely hidden in the dark earth with these old leaves over them?"

Aunt Martha, who knew so much about flowers and plants, had to admit that she didn't know that.

"May we begin to pick?" asked Nancy.

"You may each pick a small bunch," said Aunt Martha, "but be careful; they are scarce; and don't pull up any roots. We want them to come up again next year."

They were indeed scarce, but that made it even more fun to hunt for them. At last they each had as many flowers as Aunt Martha thought they should take.

"Have a few more good smells, girls," she said, "and then we'll go."

"I think," said Elsa suddenly, "that I know why mayflowers smell so sweet."

Nancy had noticed that Elsa had been quiet, as if she were thinking of something important. That usually meant she was making up a story and now they all turned to listen to her.

"I think," she said, "that the fairies have something to do with it. You see, early in the spring the Fairy Queen gives a big ball. In some ways the fairies like it even better than they do the Midsummer Eve one, because they have been shut up so long in their snow palaces. They wear their loveliest dresses, and of course they all want to put on perfumery the way ladies do when they get dressed up. They can make wonderful perfumery in Fairyland all right, but they can't get it to smell quite like Earth Spring. So in the fall when we plant bulbs and things, they go and sprinkle Fairyland perfumery on the ground where the mayflowers will grow. Then when the mayflowers come up, they smell partly Earth Spring and partly Fairy perfumery, and that is why they are sweeter than any other flowers in the world. And long before we come to pick them, even while the snow is still on the ground, the underground elves come and pick hundreds and hundreds of mayflowers and carry them through tunnels to the Fairy Queen's palace. And they decorate the palace hall with mayflowers, and the Queen and her ladies wear wreaths of mayflowers in their hair. And all Fairyland smells this wonderful, wonderful mayflower smell, and the fairies love it more than anything. And that's why mayflowers are so scarce," she finished. "The fairies have most all of them; the elves leave just a few for us."

"That's a lovely story, Elsa," said Aunt Martha. "You must write it out for me so that we can save it. Will you?"

Nancy was enchanted. "It's wonderful," she said. "Imagine a palace all decorated with mayflowers and a queen with a little wreath of mayflowers in her hair."

"I'll never, never pick too many mayflowers," said Helga. "It would be awful if there shouldn't be enough for the fairies next year."

And then at that moment something almost magic happened. It was as if the fairies had heard what Helga said and wanted to be kind to her because of her thoughtfulness. Danny had been wandering around and suddenly he gave a little bark. They looked in his direction. He did not move but barked again.

"He's found something," said Aunt Martha. "What have you got, Danny?" And they all went toward him.

"Why, it's a little gray kitten," said Sigrid, "and she looks half-starved."

"A kitten!" said Aunt Martha. "It can't be, way out here in the woods."

But it was. A tiny little kitten, all gray from the top of her head to the tip of her bedraggled-looking tail. She cried pitifully until Aunt Martha picked her up gently.

"You poor little thing! Where *have* you come from? You're nothing but a baby."

The girls crowded around. "The fairies left her for us," said Elsa.

"May we keep her at the farm?" asked Nancy.

"If nobody claims her, we will," said Aunt Martha. "At any rate, we ought to hurry home to feed her some warm milk."

"Oh, I hope nobody claims her," said Nancy. "Do you think anybody will, Aunt Martha?"

"I rather doubt it. She can't have come from the Whites' farm, because I know they don't have any young kittens."

"From the Collins'?" asked Nancy.

"Oh, no, I forgot to tell you they moved last fall and there's nobody in their place now. No, she must have come from much farther away. It's lucky you found her, Danny; she couldn't have lasted much longer."

"Oh, I hope we can keep her," the little girls kept saying as they hurried back to the farmhouse.

Aunt Martha smiled. "The way you children talk, you'd think we didn't have a single cat on the farm."

"We don't have a cat the fairies left for us," said Elsa.

"We don't have a cat that's our own special one," said Sigrid. "We ought to give her a very special name."

"An unusual name," said Elsa.

"Mayflower?" suggested Helga.

They considered this. It was a good name and unusual, but it didn't seem quite right. "It sounds more like a cow," said Sigrid.

They tried to think of all the cat names they knew; of names in storybooks; of names that would have some connection with fairies or with their mayflowering walk. Nothing seemed right. The kitten was still nameless when they carried her into the kitchen.

"First we'll feed her," said Aunt Martha. "Then dishes, and then Nancy has a surprise for you. We'll give kitty only a little milk at a time so she won't get sick, and we'll fix a little bed for her in Cicily-Ann Sinkspout's old basket."

The kitten was fed and made comfortable; the dishes were washed and put away; and then Nancy brought out Grandma's package and opened it.

"It's Grandma's *efter-kalas!*" said Sigrid. "Oh, wasn't she nice to let us have it!"

They set the table in the dining room, putting the mayflowers all in one dish in the center. Aunt Martha brought out four of her best goblets and filled them with something a lovely shade of pale pink. "It's milk colored with a little juice from some of my canned wild strawberries," she said, "to match the mayflowers."

"It's mayflower milk," said Helga.

"Don't anybody sit at the head of the table," said Aunt Martha. "We'll put something special there."

She spread a towel over the tablecloth, while the girls watched her, greatly curious. Then she went to the kitchen, lifted up the cat basket, and carried it, kitten and all, to the table.

The girls were thrilled. Their kitten right on their party table!

"Nothing like this has ever happened at an *efter-kalas* before!" said Nancy.

"No, I don't imagine it has," answered Aunt Martha, "and I don't expect it ever will again. And you must never tell that I have done such a dreadful thing—put a cat on the dining room table —but I guess it won't matter for once. It won't make a habit. I thought you'd like to have her where you can look at her while you decide on her name."

"This makes it the most wonderful *efter-kalas* in the whole world," said Nancy.

But even with the kitten right in front of them, looking so lovely and soft and gray—and already a little fatter, Sigrid said—they couldn't think of a name.

"Oh, I know," said Nancy suddenly. "We can look in the Almanac Book and give her the name for this day."

"That's a wonderful idea," said Sigrid. "A wonderful idea—oh, unless it's a boy's name today."

"If it is," said Elsa, already on her way to get Uncle Sven's Almanac, "we can add an etta or an ina to it, like Henri-etta or Joseph-ina, you know."

She came back with the book and turned to April 24. The name was Vega.

"Is that a girl's name, Aunt Martha?"

"Yes, it is."

They considered it.

"I don't like it," said Sigrid.

"Well, I don't either," said Nancy. "That kitten doesn't look a bit like Vega."

"I think Vega is also the name of a star," said Aunt Martha.

"We could call her Star," said Helga.

"*No*," said Elsa decidedly. "Anybody could think of naming a kitten Star. We want a name that's very unusual, that nobody else would ever think of."

"If I were you," said Aunt Martha, "I'd forget it for a while and before you know it the right name will pop into one of your heads."

It was in the evening when they had finished supper and were sitting around the big stove in the kitchen that Sigrid thought of the name. She was holding the kitten in her lap and suddenly she cried, "Girls, girls, I know the very name! The very one! *Cuckoo Clock*! Remember?"

Aunt Martha and Uncle Sven looked at her as if she had gone out of her wits.

"Call a cat Cuckoo Clock!" said Uncle Sven. "Well, I never. What will you think of next?"

The little girls were doubled over with laughter. They knew what Sigrid meant, but they were laughing too hard to talk.

Elsa tried. "She doesn't mean name the cat Cuckoo Clock; she . . ." but she couldn't go on.

"It's what she said," said Uncle Sven. "She said, 'I know the very name, Cuckoo Clock.'"

"But . . ." began Sigrid. "Oh, Elsa, Nancy, somebody, get the book. I don't want to disturb Cuck . . . Oh, dear, I almost *called* her Cuckoo Clock!"

This set them all off again, but Nancy and Elsa both went to the sitting room to get the book. It was a very special book indeed. After Uncle Sven had bought the farm, he had found in the attic several boxes of old books and papers, and among these the girls had discovered a book that was obviously for children. It was called *The Cuckoo Clock.* The three older girls had read it over and over and had taken turns reading it aloud to Helga. The Carlson children read it every time they came to the farm, and Nancy had been overjoyed to find a copy of it in her public library. They knew it almost by heart, and it was no wonder that they understood what Sigrid meant. The wonder was that they had not thought of it before.

Now Elsa explained to Uncle Sven and Aunt Martha. "This is what Sigrid means—it's in the beginning of the book." She read aloud:

> "A little girl in a grey merino frock and grey beaver bonnet, grey tippet and grey gloves—all grey together, even to her eyes, all except her round rosy face and bright brown hair. Her name even was rather grey, for it was Griselda."

"Griselda! It is just right," said Nancy, going

over to the kitten. "She is all in gray—see her little gray gloves; and the fur on her head is like a little gray bonnet, and she ought to have a gray name."

"Yes," said Aunt Martha, "I believe you have hit upon the name at last. The fur around her neck is even marked like a little tippet."

"Let's call her Lady Griselda Gray," said Sigrid. "It's perfect."

"It sounds like a fairy cat," said Helga.

"I don't agree," said Uncle Sven, who loved to tease the little girls. "I think she looks more as if her name should be Cuckoo Clock. That's what I'm going to call her."

"Oh, you can't," said Helga. "You can't call a cat a clock!"

"There's no law against it," said Uncle Sven.

But the little girls went to bed happily sure they had found the right name for their after-party kitten.

Early the next morning Uncle Sven opened the door at the foot of the attic stairs. "Hello, monkeys," he called. "Wake up. Cuckoo Clock seems to be fine this morning. Call her and I think she'll come upstairs."

Elsa sat up in bed. "Come on, Cuckoo Cl . . . Oh, dear, now *I* almost called her Cuckoo Clock."

This threw the little girls into giggles again.

"Cuckoo!" called Helga.

"Cuckoo!" called Sigrid.

"Cuckoo! Cuckoo! Cuckoo!" they all called until Uncle Sven warned them, "Be careful. You're scaring the poor kitten to death."

This sobered the children at once.

"I'll come right down to get her," said Nancy.

The gray kitten was really beautiful this morning. They could hardly bear to leave her when it was time to go to church.

"You darling," said Nancy, hugging her goodbye. "Lady Griselda Gray is certainly the right name for you."

It turned out that she was wrong.

Nobody ever claimed the little kitten, and nobody could find out where she came from. She grew to be the most amusing kitten that ever lived on the farm. She was a real little clown of a cat. She was always getting into mischief; there was no end to the funny things she thought of doing. It was impossible to call such a comical little clown Lady Griselda Gray or even just Griselda. Nancy held out longest, but at last even she had to give in and admit that Uncle Sven was right. The absurd name the after-party cat got quite by accident fitted her much better.

She lived to be an old, old lady cat, but even

when she was a dignified grandmother with children and grandchildren running about the farm, she was never called anything but Cuckoo Clock.

"Well, you have to admit," the girls used to say to each other now and then, "it's a *very* unusual name for a cat. Nobody else would ever have thought of it!"

Chapter 5

THE COLORED WINDOW

NANCY had now been with the Bensons only three days and there had already been two parties—the name day at Grandma's and the *efter-kalas* at Aunt Martha's. The afternoon at Aunt Anna's when everybody helped to make the May basket seemed almost like a party, too; so that made three in three days!

"It's the way things always are when I visit Grandma," thought Nancy. "I wonder if it will be like this every single day all spring and summer."

Even the papering of Nancy's room turned into a kind of party, although it was hard work.

Aunt Anna and Aunt Martha came to help because they thought Grandma ought not to do it alone with only Nancy to help her; and the Carlson girls came after school so they would have a part in it, too. The hardest work was getting the old paper off and scrubbing the walls. When the time came to put on the new paper, it was only fun. The room, Nancy thought, looked more beautiful with every strip that was hung, and on the day when the papering was finished, she could hardly wait for school to be over so that Sigrid and Elsa and Helga could see it. When they did, they loved the yellow roses as much as she did and at once began to have all kinds of wonderful ideas.

Sigrid remembered that Aunt Anna had a piece of yellow muslin and suggested that maybe Nancy could have it to make bands to tie back the white curtains. "There are four girls and Nancy'll need four bands," said Elsa, "so why can't we have a sewing party and each hem a tieback?" The muslin proved to match the roses perfectly, and the sewing party was great fun. To be sure, the stitches were rather large and uneven, but who cared about stitches when the yellow was such a lovely color and the roses were so gay?

Grandma said that she would help Nancy braid

a chair seat for the gray-green rocker, and she let Nancy choose strips for it from her piece bag. Nancy found gray and green ones; there were no yellow. Then Elsa suggested that she spend ten cents of the money her Papa had given her for a piece of yellow cambric to cut into strips and braid in here and there; and that made the chair seat perfect. Nancy was proud of it.

Grandma told her she might invite one of the Carlson girls to spend the night with her each Friday until they had all had a turn at sleeping in the yellow-rose room. The girls drew lots to see in which order they should come. First came Helga, then Sigrid, then Elsa. Those were three gay Friday nights.

But there were lonely times, too, when Nancy felt she couldn't get along without Mamma and Papa another day. It never took Grandma long to discover that Nancy was homesick, and she would often drop whatever she was doing, sit down in the kitchen rocking chair, and take Nancy on her lap. Sometimes they would sit quietly without talking; sometimes Grandma would tell about her childhood in Sweden or about the days when Nancy's mother was a little girl and used to play with Anna and Martha and the other children.

Sometimes they would talk about name days, for Nancy could not get them out of her mind. She could not have told why it seemed so important to her to have one. Grandma was giving her so many good times she should have been satisfied, but she couldn't help wishing and wishing for a name day.

Everybody—grownups and children—kept trying to think of ways to get her one, but it proved to be much harder than anyone had supposed it would be. None of the grownups could think of a way. The children at least had ideas. Even little Helga had one.

"I know what you could do, Nancy," she said. "You could have a name day party for Charlotte. I know she has a name day because our Aunt Charlotte does—it's on the twelfth of May."

"That's a wonderful idea," said Elsa. "We could make a tiny flower crown for her and decorate the house and dress up all the dolls with garlands of flowers."

"And make a tiny name day cake," said Sigrid.

But it didn't help Nancy. "It would be a lovely party," she said, "but it wouldn't be *my* name day."

Elsa had a friend whom she decided to consult.

His name was Mr. Sanborn, and he lived around the corner from the Carlsons.

"We got to be friends," she explained with great satisfaction to Nancy, "because we are both bookworms. He has more books than you could ever imagine one person having, and sometimes he invites me to come in to read them. He'd let me come oftener but Mamma won't; she thinks I bother him. But maybe she'll let you and me go today."

Aunt Anna said they might if they would stay only a few minutes.

"This seems like a story," said Nancy, as they went up Mr. Sanborn's front steps, "where we are going to consult the Wise Man because nobody else knows the answer."

Mr. Sanborn came to the door.

"This is Nancy Bruce," said Elsa, "and she's a bookworm, too."

Mr. Sanborn shook hands with Nancy.

"Always glad to meet another bookworm," he said. "And what can I do for you two ladies today? Would you like to come in and browse around a bit?"

"We have come to you for help," said Elsa, "when all else has failed."

"Dear me," said Mr. Sanborn, "what in the

world is the matter? You'd better come in to explain."

They went in and Elsa told all about name days and the Swedish Almanac that didn't have any Nancy in it.

Mr. Sanborn was immensely interested.

"I have always been fascinated by names," said he. "In fact, I've made quite a study of them. Let me think a minute."

He leaned back in his chair and shut his eyes. They waited.

Suddenly he opened his eyes and sat up straight.

"I think perhaps Nancy is in the Almanac," he said, "only it is there in disguise."

This was certainly a surprising answer.

"Goodness," said Elsa, "Nancy said this was like coming to consult a Wise Man in a story; and that sounds like the kind of answer the Wise Man would give. But what does it mean?"

"Is Anne in the Swedish Almanac?" asked Mr. Sanborn.

"I don't know, but Anna is."

"Then there's your answer. Did you know that some people who are christened Anne or Anna are called Nancy for a nickname? Just as some people who are christened Elizabeth may be called Betsy or Lizzie; or sometimes Elsa. Did you know that Elsa may be a nickname for Elizabeth?"

Elsa was almost indignant. "Not in Swedish, it isn't, I bet," she said. "Elsa's *Elsa* and Elizabeth's *Elizabeth*. I *know* because Mamma has a friend named Elizabeth and her name and mine are both in the Almanac and not on the same day at all."

Nancy was just as decided in her opinion. "And I wasn't christened Anne or Anna," she said. "I was christened Nancy. I couldn't have Anna for a name day. It isn't my *name*."

"It's plain to see that I too have failed," said Mr. Sanborn. "I'm very sorry."

"Oh, you couldn't help it," said Elsa, "and you haven't had much time to think. You might get a good idea. If you do, will you please let us know?"

Mr. Sanborn promised that he would, and the children thanked him and left. They were disappointed and puzzled.

But suddenly Elsa began to giggle. "Do you know who this is walking down the street?" she said. "This is Miss Anna Bruce and Miss Elizabeth Carlson."

They looked at each other and began to laugh. They were still giggling when they got home, and Sigrid and Helga, who had been waiting anxiously, thought surely Mr. Sanborn had found a name day. When they heard what had happened, Sigrid was disgusted.

"I don't think Mr. Sanborn is as smart as you make out, Elsa," she said.

"Oh, yes he *is*," said Elsa. "He's going to think some more and maybe he'll have an idea."

But even Mr. Sanborn, with all his books, couldn't think of a name day to satisfy Nancy.

"Poor child," said Aunt Anna one rainy Saturday afternoon, as she and Aunt Martha sat sewing with Grandma in the kitchen, while the children were playing in Nancy's room upstairs. "I thought it was going to be easy to find some way to get a name day for her, but nothing anybody suggests satisfies her. It's partly that she's homesick, I suppose. She's been with her mother and father so constantly and they've played with her so much that it's pretty hard to be separated from them even if she is having a good time."

"And she's found out how much we make of name days in this family," said Aunt Martha. "I know some Swedish families who don't even think of them any more now that they've got to America."

"Well, they ought to," said Grandma, "the children love them so."

"Oh, I know it," said Aunt Martha. "The name day parties you have given us all are among our happiest memories. And then, too, there is something special about one's own name. I remember how I always used to love to have Papa tell me stories about a little girl named Martha. I can understand how Nancy feels about not wanting any substitute for her own name. But whatever we're going to do about it, I don't know. I didn't realize how hard it was going to be."

"No, I didn't either," said Grandma. "Poor little one! I only hope the *children* can think of something finally. We've practically promised her a name day, and now we don't seem to be able to keep our promise."

It was while this conversation was going on downstairs that Sigrid suddenly had her great idea upstairs.

"Say, kids," she cried, "I just thought of something. We must be dumb not to have thought of it before. Nancy's got a middle name! Why can't she have a name day party on that day? Wouldn't that be all right, Nancy? It's just exactly as much your own name as your first one is!"

Nancy was overjoyed. Her middle name was Wanda. It was an unusual and romantic name, chosen because Mamma had read it in a story and liked it. Nancy had always wished it had been given to her as a first name. Nancy, she thought, wasn't half so beautiful. To have a Wanda Day would be simply wonderful.

The little girls rushed downstairs into the kitchen for the Almanac. Excitedly they explained the great idea to the grownups and then plunged into the book. From January through December they went carefully, day by day, name by name. In all the Almanac there was no Wanda.

"If that isn't the meanest thing I ever heard of!" said Elsa. "To leave both your names out! Who made this old Almanac anyway?"

But of course they knew it wasn't anybody's fault. It was only that Wanda wasn't a Swedish name either.

"It sounds like one, though," said Sigrid. "Nancy doesn't, but Wanda sounds as Swedish as Elsa or Anna or Helga."

Nancy was so disappointed that she burst into tears. The other girls were all sympathy. "Oh, don't cry, Nancy. Don't cry. *Please!* We'll all think some more."

"Yes, we'll think some more, dear," said Aunt Anna, taking out her handkerchief and wiping Nancy's eyes. But Grandma, who always thought there was no cure for trouble like a good party, said, "We'll have a party anyway. Right now! Whose name day is it today? We'll celebrate it whosever it is. I'll get out my mixing bowl and make some *plätter*, and we'll have *plätter* and coffee right in the middle of Saturday afternoon! We'll show that old name day book! See whose name day it is, girls."

Plätter were a kind of Swedish pancake that the children loved, and nobody could make them better than Grandma could. Elsa looked up the date in the Almanac. The name was Åke.

"What a funny name!" she said. "I never heard of it."

"Well, think of that," said Grandma, "Åke! I know that name all right. Once upon a time I had a little pig for a pet and his name was Åke."

Aunt Anna and Aunt Martha looked at each other in surprise, but the children were paying attention only to Grandma.

"It *was*!" said Sigrid. "How did you ever happen to think of giving the pig that name?"

"Because it was the name of the farmer who gave me the pig," said Grandma, and went on to tell the children what a cunning little pig it was and how it had followed her everywhere just like a dog. And how she had knitted a little stocking cap out of odds and ends of colored yarn and how comical Åke had looked wearing it. "And it's about time we celebrated his name day!" she finished. And even Nancy had to forget her own name day and giggle at the thought of eating *plätter* and drinking coffee in the middle of Saturday afternoon in honor of a pig!

"I know what," said Sigrid, "if I could have a piece of bundle paper or newspaper, I could draw and cut out a pig and a lot of stocking caps and after we eat the *plätter* we could play, not pin the tail on the donkey, but pin the stocking cap on Åke."

"This must be the funniest name day party that ever came out of the Almanac," said Aunt Martha.

And so once more Nancy forgot for a little while how much she wanted a name day of her own. But something was always happening to remind her.

The time drew near when she and Grandpa were to make the best name day cake in the world. She began to feel worried, but one day Grandpa told her a secret. It was such a good joke that he and she laughed every time they looked at each other in the next few days, and Grandma and the Carlson girls realized that this was to be no ordinary name day cake. The girls could hardly contain themselves for curiosity. But Grandpa and Nancy kept their secret.

Erik Day came in the middle of the week when Grandpa had to work, so the party was to be given Sunday noon instead, and the name day cake was to be the dessert. The whole Carlson family was to come to dinner after church and Sunday School.

Nancy and Grandpa got up early in the morning and would not let Grandma come near the kitchen, after she had finished her breakfast, until they had their work there done. When she did come out, she sniffed as if she were trying to smell something. "I can't smell that any cake has been baking," she said. Grandpa and Nancy looked more mysterious than ever.

Dinnertime came and at last the time for the cake to be served. Grandpa and Nancy got up from the table, went to the kitchen, and shut the door between the kitchen and the dining room. In a few minutes they came back, and Grandpa was carrying, not a cake plate, but Grandma's biggest cake pan! It was filled to the brim with something pink, decorated with red. The Carlson girls couldn't sit still; they had to jump up and come and look more closely.

The red was strawberries—lovely big strawber-

ries, the first of the season. With them Nancy
had spelled out:

ERIK DAY   MAY 18

And the pink . . .

"Why, it isn't cake at all. It's ICE CREAM!"
cried Sigrid.

Ice cream—that was something the children
had only on very, very special occasions. On
Fourth of July, always, and perhaps three or four
other times a year. And now Nancy and Grandpa
had made some in the freezer that was kept for
these special occasions. And put fresh strawberries in the ice cream and on it, too!

"What do you mean, it isn't cake?" asked
Grandpa. "It's in a cake pan, isn't it? What do
you think, Nancy? Doesn't it look to you like
a cake? Of course if nobody here likes it, we can
give it away and go out in the kitchen and make
a sponge cake or something."

By this time the little girls were tugging at his
arms to get his attention. "No, no, Grandpa! No,
it's the best, the most wonderful name day cake
in the world. It's *much* better than sponge cake!"

"Well, I'm relieved to hear it," said Grandpa.
"Then I don't have to eat my best straw hat?"

"No, no," they all shouted.

"Come on," said Nancy, "let's eat the ice c—I mean the cake—then."

"That's the best idea yet," said Grandpa.

After dinner the ladies did the dishes and Grandpa and Uncle John, Sigrid and Elsa and Helga's father, took the little girls for a long walk in the woods, and when they came back, there was another surprise. A second dish of ice cream for everybody!

Of course there were many days when Nancy and Grandma were alone almost all day. Then Nancy played with Oscar or Teddy; or with her paper dolls or Charlotte; or helped Grandma with the housework and cooking; or answered her letters from Mamma and Papa.

And she spent many hours reading. Grandpa let her take his library card, and she read all the books she could borrow, and the ones the Carlson girls borrowed on their cards, too. One day Aunt Martha, when she came to bring eggs for the store, brought also *The Cuckoo Clock* and said Nancy might keep it for a week.

Nancy was delighted and didn't even stay to hear what Grandma and Aunt Martha might have to say while they were drinking their coffee. In-

stead she took the book and went out into the front hall to sit halfway up the stairs to read. Nancy loved this hall, principally because high up over the stairs was a colored glass window, rather like a church window. It had a pane of frosted glass in the middle and smaller panes of color in a border around the frosted part. Blue and gold and violet, green and crimson were the colors. Nancy thought it was beautiful.

And now she discovered something enchanting. She made herself comfortable on the landing, where the stairway turned, and opened her book to read. She chose her favorite part—where Griselda, dressed in her nightgown, enters the cuckoo clock for the first time, and the cuckoo, thinking she may be cold, gives her a little cloak to wear. A little cloak made of feathers and lined with red velvet.

> ". . . feathers of every shade and colour, but beautifully worked in, somehow, so as to lie quite smoothly and evenly, one colour melting away into another like those in a prism, so that you could hardly tell where one began and another ended."

And just as Nancy was reading this, the sun, which had hidden behind the clouds most of the day, suddenly burst forth, and, shining through the window, colored the pages of the book. It was a little old book with small type and hardly any pictures, but now it had become enchanted. By moving a little Nancy could change the colors so that the pages became blue and golden, crimson and green and violet as she read. It was like reading a book in Fairyland. She had never imagined any book so lovely. And to think that this had happened to her favorite, *Cuckoo Clock*! It was as if the cuckoo had enchanted her as well as Griselda.

When Aunt Martha called to say goodbye, Nancy was as startled as if she had suddenly been called out of Fairyland.

Over and over again that week, when the sun was shining, Nancy took *The Cuckoo Clock* to read on the stairs. She never read any other book there; she never told anyone else about the wonder of the adventure. There seemed to be no words to tell it—it belonged to her and to Griselda and the cuckoo.

And so the days went by and most of them were happy. But years later, as Nancy looked back on that spring and summer, she realized that five enchanted days stood out more clearly in her memory than did any of the others. It was as if the sunlight had played on them as it did on *The Cuckoo Clock* through the colored panes of the window.

Chapter 6

THE APPLE ORCHARD

WHEN it was time for the apple trees to blossom, Nancy went to the farm. The first two days of her week there were cold and rainy, but on the third morning the sun shone and the sky was so blue that she said when she came down to breakfast, "This is about the bluest day I ever saw. Look at the sky, Aunt Martha."

"Yes, I've already noticed how blue it is," said Aunt Martha, "and that's good because I want to wash the dresses that I persuaded Grandma to let me do up for you. It is such a good drying day that maybe I can get them both washed and ironed this morning."

Nancy looked up at the sky again. "It can't possibly rain today," she said, "not with that blue sky. Aunt Martha, I think I like blue better than any color except yellow. It's so—so *blue!*"

Aunt Martha laughed. "Then you'll be pleased at a little surprise I have for you," she said. "Come eat your breakfast, and later on I'll show you."

"A blue surprise, Aunt Martha? What is it?"

"You wait. I'll show it to you when the washing is all done and I get to the ironing. That is— if you'll do the breakfast dishes for me and run around the henyard three times with Danny and cut out some cookies while I iron. Will you do all that?"

"Oh, yes!" said Nancy. "Oh, yes! Could I cut the cookies with the fancy cutters? Please?"

"You certainly may," said Aunt Martha.

Nancy sat down to eat her breakfast, but she had not even had time to take her napkin out of its ring before three cats came to sit near her chair and look hopefully up at her. They were Cicily-Ann Sinkspout, the oldest cat on the farm; Cuckoo Clock, the youngest; and a stray cat who had arrived only a few days before and made himself completely at home. "Blacky, the Howling Success," Aunt Martha called him, and you didn't have to know him long to understand why.

"Merr-ou-ou-w," he said now. "Merr-OUW!"

"Listen to him," said Aunt Martha. "It was bad enough when Cicily-Ann Sinkspout begged at the table, but now they're all at it. Even Cuckoo Clock. Though why any cat in this house or in Grandma's should beg for food, I don't know. It must be that they enjoy the sociability while you're eating. Give them each a tiny piece of buttered muffin and that's all. You don't want to kill them with kindness."

"Is there any coffee left?" asked Nancy. "Could I give them each a little coffee the way I do Teddy?"

"No, ma'am!" said Aunt Martha decidedly. "Grandma has only one cat, remember, but there are seven here on the farm. And if you think I'm going to let you get them into bad habits so that I have to set out coffee with cream and sugar for seven cats every morning, you've got another think coming."

Nancy giggled. "Someday you could let each cat invite a friend," she said, "and make a real party of it."

"Get along with you," said Aunt Martha, laughing. "We're both foolish enough about animals as it is. Eat your breakfast now and I'll shoo

100

these animals outdoors or we'll never get any work done."

It did not take Nancy long to eat or to do the dishes and she soon had her sweater on, ready to go out to play with Danny.

"Your rubbers, too," said Aunt Martha. "It's still wet in the grass."

Danny was a hard-working farm dog, but he liked his fun, too; and his favorite game was one in which the children ran round and round the large henyard with him.

"One, two, three! One, two, three! Run around the henyard, Danny and me!" they would call, and he would tear off around the fenced-in yard and be back at the starting point before the children were halfway around. Why this seemed so much fun to him nobody knew, but as soon as one of the children came out of the farmhouse door, he would run to the corner of the henyard and wait for the race to begin. And if any child tried to turn back instead of going all the way around, Danny would be after him immediately, steering him in the right direction.

"All right, Danny," Nancy said now, going toward him. "One, two, three! One, two, three! Run around the henyard, Danny and me!"

They were off. But Nancy got only halfway

101

round—the henyard bordered on the edge of the orchard and she could go no farther. She had to stop to smell the sweetness of the apple blossoms this lovely May morning. As far as she could see down through the orchard, there was nothing but pink and white trees. "It's beautiful," she said to herself. "It's just beautiful." But Danny was not interested in orchards; she could hear him barking, up at the starting point of the race.

"I'm coming, I'm coming, Danny," she called, but she couldn't move. The apple trees, after the rain, were so fresh, and the air was so sweet. Danny had to come to get her, barking wildly all the way, but when he reached her and she put her arm around him, he stood patiently beside her.

"Isn't it beautiful, Danny?" she said at last. "You were a good dog to wait for me and now I'll run with you."

Three times they went around the yard, and when they had finished, Aunt Martha was coming out with the basket of clothes in her arms.

Nancy helped to hang out her dresses—her pink-and-white-checked gingham, her red-and-green-plaid jumper and the white blouse that belonged with it, her blue linen sailor suit, and her best dress that Aunt Marion had made for her.

That was Nancy's favorite. It was white, with lace on the skirt, and a special kind of lace, called beading, around the neck and little puffed sleeves. The beading had eyelets through which Aunt Marion had threaded pink ribbon that tied in bows on the sleeves and at the neck. The dress had a pink sash, too. It was her party dress and she wore it only on the most special occasions. The ribbon was always taken out when the dress was washed, so it was all white now, and soon it would be dry and stiff with starch and Aunt Martha would iron it. It was a lot of extra work for her to do up all these dresses, but she never seemed rushed.

"Let's walk down in the orchard before we go in the house again," she said. "It's too lovely to miss. No, Danny, Nancy isn't going to run around the henyard again. You come with us." So the three went down among the blossoming trees together.

"I don't know which I like best," said Aunt Martha, "the apple trees in blossom in the spring, or the colored leaves of the maples in the fall, or the evergreen when it makes the whole house smell Christmas."

Nancy skipped along beside her. "Just now I like the apple trees best," she said. For almost half an hour they wandered in and out among them, and Nancy thought she had never known such a beautiful morning.

"Now we have had a treat," said Aunt Martha, "we'll give one to Uncle Sven, too. He's plowing in the north field. I'll make some coffee and we'll take it over to him."

Although they did not walk through the orchard to get to the north field, they could still smell the blossoms all the way.

"I love the smell of the plowed earth, too," said Nancy when they had given Uncle Sven his coffee, and she looked so happy that he patted her lovingly on the head. "You're a real little farmer, Nancy," he said.

When Aunt Martha and Nancy got back to the farmhouse, the dresses were dry. Aunt Martha sprinkled them and then mixed the cooky batter. Nancy washed her hands and put on a clean apron. She went to the drawer where the cooky cutters were kept. First she took out her favorite. It was a Teddy bear. She had never seen one anywhere else and none of her friends had ever heard of one. The Carlson girls and their friends had never heard of one either. As far as they could discover, Aunt Martha was the only person in the world who had a Teddy bear cooky cutter. Nancy chose also a star-shaped cutter and a heart and a

clover leaf, and a round one with scalloped edges. All these cookies she would cut, and the Teddy bears she would decorate with currants so they would look like proper bears. The next hour was a busy one, but at the end of it the cookies were baking in the oven and the dresses were ironed.

"Now," said Aunt Martha, "while I get dinner you can fix your blue surprise."

"*Fix* my surprise?" asked Nancy. "What do you mean?"

Aunt Martha went into the sitting room and brought back a small package.

"Your Aunt Marion sent me a dollar to buy this for your party dress. She thought you might think it was fun to change colors. Sometimes you can use the pink ribbon and sometimes this."

Nancy opened the package. In it were several yards of blue ribbon for the beading and enough wider ribbon of the same shade for a sash and hair ribbons.

"Oh, it's lovely," said Nancy. "It's lovely and blue. It will be like having two different dresses. May I put the ribbon in the beading right now and could I cut off a tiny piece to send Mamma so she can see it?"

"Yes, you could cut off a piece long enough for

her to use for a bookmark. I'm sure there'll be plenty."

Nancy went to Aunt Martha's sewing basket and got the large-eyed needle called a bodkin and sat down to thread the ribbon through the beading. It looked beautiful when it was done. She carried the dress up to her room, but even before dinner she had to run up again several times to look at it.

Soon Uncle Sven came in. "I'm hungry enough to eat a horse," he said.

"Well, we didn't make any horses," said Nancy, "but we did make bears. Will they do?"

Uncle Sven examined them all carefully. "I'll take that one," he said. "He has a wicked look in his eye; I think it would be better to put him out of the way soon."

The cookies were dessert for dinner. Uncle Sven said they were so good that one bear was not nearly enough; he must have one each of every other kind, too.

By afternoon the day was as warm as summer.

"Let's sit on the front porch," said Aunt Martha. "I have some mending I must do and I'll take it out there and enjoy the weather. Why don't you take your work out there, too?"

"Goody, I will," said Nancy.

Now she had to decide what to do. There were so many possibilities that it was hard to choose. She could take her paper and crayons and make new clothes for her paper doll families. Or she could cut out furniture from the cardboard sheets she and the Carlson girls had bought at Miss Dilly's store. Nancy had a dining room, a kitchen, and a bedroom. Each sheet cost one cent, and as soon as Papa sent her a little more spending money she could buy a parlor, too. The furniture was the right size to go into a little dollhouse made from two shoe boxes.

Or she could work on the bureau scarf she was making for her yellow-rose room. The scarf had come from Miss Dilly's shop, too. It was white and it was to be embroidered with white daisies with yellow centers and green stems and leaves. It was exciting to work on it.

Or she could make clothes for Jasmine. Jasmine was about three inches high, and she had three cousins whose mothers were Sigrid and Elsa and Helga. Papa had sent the four little dolls only last week. Elsa had suggested that they name them all for flowers; that was why Nancy had chosen Jasmine. She had never seen any jasmine flowers, but she had read about them in a story and she loved the sound of the name. Sigrid had decided

on Marigold for her doll and Helga had chosen
Daisy. Elsa had looked through the wildflower
book in her room at school and announced that
her daughter's name was to be Trillium. Sigrid
was disgusted, but she couldn't help laughing.

"That isn't a girl's name," she said.

"It's my girl's name," said Elsa.

So those were their names: Jasmine, Daisy,
Marigold, and Trillium.

Nancy decided that this afternoon she would
make clothes for Jasmine. She got her doll and
her sewing box and the cloth Grandma had given
her and went out on the porch to wait for Aunt
Martha. The afternoon was as lovely as the morning had been, with the scent of apple blossoms
and syringas and the newly budded lilacs; and
the grass so fresh and green and the sky so blue.

Aunt Martha came to the front door. "Nancy,"
she said, "why don't you go upstairs and put on
your best party dress?"

Nancy looked at her in surprise. "Is there going
to be a party?"

"No," Aunt Martha answered, "I only thought
it might be fun to dress up in your best dress."

Nancy's look of surprise changed to one of
complete astonishment.

"But you just washed and ironed it," she said.

"Do you mean I could put it on just to wear sitting on the front steps with nobody here but you and me?"

"Why not?" said Aunt Martha. "Sometimes it makes you feel good to dress up in a best dress. Don't you want to?"

"Oh, yes, I want to all right," said Nancy. "I want to very much, but I never wore a best dress before unless there was a party or something. Why, at home I even have to take off my school dress and put on my play one when I get home in the afternoon."

"And a good idea, too," said Aunt Martha, "but once in a while it's fun to do something different for a change."

"I'll put it on right off," said Nancy, suddenly warming to the idea. "And can I unbraid my hair and have it hanging and will you tie one of my new ribbons around it?"

"I will," said Aunt Martha, "and I'll put on my best dress, too."

They went into the house.

"What a wonderful day this is," said Nancy.

She put on her best petticoat and changed her shoes and stockings. She scrubbed her face and hands and unbraided her hair. It was a little wavy because it had been braided so tightly. Nancy sighed; she knew well enough that before the afternoon was over every hair would be straight. But even that didn't worry her much this exciting day. Aunt Martha was ready before Nancy was. She had put on her last summer's blue muslin dress and looked lovely. She helped Nancy slip on her dress, tied the sash and put the ribbon on her hair.

They went out on the porch again. Nancy felt as if she were in a dream.

"You were right," she said to Aunt Martha, "putting on a best dress does make you feel good; it makes you feel very, very good. I don't feel like me; I think I'm a girl in a storybook. Maybe I'm a princess. Oh, isn't it *fun!*"

It was fun to sit there in the afternoon sunshine, sewing and talking and feeling dressed up and special. Every once in a while Nancy laughed out of sheer delight. "This is one of the nicest days I have ever had in all my whole, whole life," she said.

When it was time to get supper, Aunt Martha tied an apron over her best dress and another over Nancy's. But before Uncle Sven came to the table they took their aprons off so that he would see how dressed up they were.

He was surprised. "Well, my goodness," he

said, "what's going on here? Has there been a party? Why have you got on your best dresses?"

"There hasn't been a party," said Nancy, "but sometimes it makes you feel good to dress up."

"Is that so?" said Uncle Sven. "Then I'd better dress up, too."

He went out of the house and down toward the orchard. Nancy ran to see what he was going to do. He went to the only apple tree from which they picked any blossoms. The apples on that tree were never very good; so Aunt Martha said they would at least enjoy the blossoms as flowers. Uncle Sven picked two sprigs and stuck one behind each ear, holding them in place with the bows of his glasses. He looked so funny—as if apple blossoms were growing right out of his ears!

There was a bouquet of blossoms on the dining room table and Aunt Martha had used her best dishes. What a wonderful, wonderful day!

And even this wasn't the end of it.

Later in the evening when the moon had come up, Aunt Martha opened the door that looked down toward the orchard.

"Nancy," she said, "come look at the orchard by moonlight."

Nancy ran to the door.

"I will stand here on the piazza," said Aunt

Martha, "while you run way down in the orchard all by yourself."

"All by myself? Couldn't you come, too?"

"No, you go all by yourself—way down into the heart of the orchard. I'll be right here watching you. There's nothing to be afraid of. Run along."

"I'm not afraid," said Nancy, and went toward the orchard.

No, she was not afraid, but this was certainly a most surprising day! To go out all by herself at night! She began to run. She ran until she was right in the middle of the orchard. There were apple blossoms all around her; she was even walking on some of the fallen petals. It was like being in a house made entirely of pink and white flowers. No, it wasn't like being in a house at all—it was like being out-of-doors in a world made of apple blossoms. Now Nancy could not run any more. She hardly wanted to walk or even to breathe. The moon shining down on the orchard made it even lovelier than it had been in the daytime—with a kind of loveliness Nancy had never known before.

It was wonderful to be all alone in a world of apple blossoms. Suddenly she noticed how white her dress looked in the moonlight—it was a shim-

mering white. She put her hand up and touched her hair, half-wondering if it might have turned curly and golden. She began to walk on tiptoe from tree to tree, stopping to look up into each one. She held out her arms as if to gather in all the loveliness. Then slowly she turned and walked back to the house.

Aunt Martha was waiting for her, and Nancy went up on the piazza to stand beside her and look once more at all the beauty she had just been a part of.

"Once when I was a little girl about your age," said Aunt Martha, "Grandpa let me go out in a blossoming apple orchard all alone in the moonlight. I have always remembered."

"I will remember, too," said Nancy.

And together they went into the lamplit kitchen.

Chapter 7

THE BIRCH GATHERERS

ANOTHER of the days Nancy was always to remember came during that same week. It was the
day they all went with Grandma to gather the
birch twigs which she made into little round
whisk brooms for herself and her friends to use
for beating gravies, eggs, and puddings. Swedish
ladies felt that these little whisk brooms were far
superior to modern egg beaters.

"The whisks beat things so that they are
smoother and creamier," said Grandma. "And,
besides, they give everything a flavor of springtime."

Nancy could barely remember going on a

birch-gathering expedition one other year; it must have been when she was four or five. That time they had gone to a wood near Grandma's house, but this year Grandma had decided to come to the farm instead. She would wait until Saturday so that Aunt Anna and the girls could come, too. With Aunt Martha and Nancy they would make the right size of crowd for a spring birch tree party.

There was only one thing to worry about—the weather. If it was rainy, they couldn't go to the woods, and Grandma was afraid the following Saturday would be too late. "I usually gather the twigs even earlier," she said. "I don't know where the spring has gone. We need to pick the twigs before they get too stiff and tough. If we don't, they won't beat things right." So it was important that Saturday should be a fair day.

It was important for more than one reason. It so happened that the day they were going birch gathering was Grandma's birthday and the little girls had been planning several surprises. They had been talking about the party for a long time, but from Friday morning on Nancy could talk of nothing else. As soon as she was dressed that morning, she ran outdoors.

"It gets lovelier every day," she reported when

119

she came back. "Oh, if it's only like this tomorrow! The lilacs are way out and there are more red tulips in blossom and I saw a bluebird in the apple orchard and a bird with gold on it in a lilac bush and the Japanese quince is almost out and down by the old well the violets are blue as blue."

She stopped, but only because she was out of breath.

Aunt Martha smiled at her. "You do love the country, don't you, Nancy?"

"Yes, I do," Nancy answered, "but I never saw it like this. When I came to Grandma's, it was a gray day, and now look! It's the way Grandpa said it would be. He said it would be a beautiful thing to see the world turning from grayness into all the colors of springtime. And it is. I never saw spring coming before, and I didn't know exactly what he meant. But now I do."

Aunt Martha looked at her, suddenly understanding. "I never thought of that. A little girl who lives right in the heart of the city doesn't see spring come, does she?"

"Well, not like this anyway," said Nancy. "Of course Mamma has pansies in our window boxes, and the flower carts come and they are beautiful and we take walks to the park on Sunday, but it's never like this. Here there's something different every minute! And it's so—so MUCH! And the air seems different—everything seems so *happy*. Oh, I hope it will be like this tomorrow. Isn't it wonderful that Grandma has her birthday this very Saturday!

"Aunt Martha, do all Swedish ladies go out in the spring to get birch branches?"

"A good many of them still do; but years ago, when Grandma was a little girl in Sweden and they couldn't get things like egg beaters, they had to make their own. That's why she loves to now, I think."

"And did they make it a holiday?"

"No, I don't think they actually made it a holiday, but very often they went out to get the birches—a big group of people all together—because they were glad it was spring. But you know Grandma—she makes a festival out of everything. When I was little, we always looked forward to the day. Sometimes there would be only Grandma and we children in the birch woods, and we were poor and didn't have much for a treat, but that didn't matter. As long as Grandma was there it was a party anyway."

"She loves Sweden, doesn't she?" said Nancy.

"Yes. You see she was eighteen when she came to America. Grandpa and Uncle Sven were so little when they came that they hardly remember Sweden, but Grandma spent all her childhood and young girlhood there. Suppose you came to this farm every spring until you were eighteen and then went to another country and could never see the farm again. Wouldn't you still love it and think of it often?"

Nancy was aghast. "Never, never see this farm again!" she said.

"Or Grandma's house or your own house or Sigrid or Elsa or Helga or any of us," said Aunt Martha. "That's the way it was with Grandma and lots of the people who came from Europe. They left behind everything they loved. No wonder they think of it often and are lonely sometimes."

It was too much for Nancy. She couldn't imagine what it would be like. She looked so troubled that Aunt Martha said, "Come, don't look so sad. Grandma's glad she came to America even if she does love Sweden, too. But we'd better get going or we'll not have the birch tree birthday ready."

It was a busy day, but by bedtime the house was spick-and-span; coffee bread had been baked and the birthday cake was ready for the girls to frost the next day. Aunt Anna would bring cookies.

Before Nancy went upstairs, she looked anxiously out of the kitchen door. "The stars are out," she said to Uncle Sven. "Does that mean for sure that it will be clear tomorrow?"

"Well, it might change in the night," he said, "but I don't think it will. I'm pretty sure you'll have a good day."

Nancy had raised the window shade in her bedroom so that she could see what the weather was the minute she woke up in the morning. It was perfect. She hopped out of bed, put on her robe and slippers, ran downstairs, snatched up Cuckoo Clock, who was sitting by the stove, and began to dance round and round the kitchen, singing:

"It's a lovely, lovely day, Cuckoo Clock, Cuckoo Clock! It's a lovely, lovely day, Cuckoo Clock!

"Oh, Aunt Martha, isn't it perfectly, perfectly wonderful!"

She put a rather surprised Cuckoo Clock down on the floor and went to wash her face and hands and get ready for breakfast.

"Would you like to be the flower gatherer all yourself?" asked Aunt Martha. "I have so much to do that it would be a great help if you would take entire charge of the decorating. We want the house to look nice for Grandma's birthday."

"I'd love to be the flower gatherer," said Nancy.

"Good! Uncle Sven picked some of the blossoms from the old apple tree before he went to town. They are in a pail of water in the shed. The rest of the picking you may do yourself."

Nancy spent a long time gathering the flowers and then went from room to room, trying a bowl of violets here, a bunch of lilacs there, pansies, quince, and apple blossoms first in one place and then in another.

"Only fifteen minutes more," said Aunt Martha finally. "You know you promised to lie down to rest for an hour."

"I'm not a bit tired."

"You think so now, but you'd better rest anyway so that you won't be too tired later."

Nancy hurried to decide about her flowers. The violets she put in a glass bowl on the dining room table; a dish of purple and yellow pansies seemed right for the sitting room table. On the floor in the sitting room she set a big pitcher. She had to carry water in a smaller pitcher to fill it and when it was ready, she arranged white and purple lilacs in it. On the kitchen table, where Uncle Sven kept his newspapers and his reading lamp, she put a vase with a few branches of flame-colored quince; and a big crock on the front porch she filled with apple blossoms. She saved a few of these blossoms for a special surprise Aunt Martha had thought of.

"Time's up!" said Aunt Martha. "You have done a fine job and everything looks lovely. Run upstairs and lie down until I call you."

"Please may I take Cuckoo Clock up with me?"

"No, she'll be so lively she'll keep you from resting. But Cicily-Ann Sinkspout is out on the porch. You may take her; if she stays at all, she'll lie still."

Cicily-Ann Sinkspout was willing to oblige, so she and Nancy lay and rested together.

"You're another one with a funny name," Nancy said to her as she tickled her gently back of her ears.

Nancy knew how that funny name had come about. Uncle Sven and Aunt Martha had only one cat when they lived in the city. That cat was Cicily-Ann. When Uncle Sven bought the farm, he said to her, "Now you will have to work, Cicily-Ann. It will be up to you to keep the buildings free of mice." But Cicily-Ann found something else to do.

In the kitchen sink, at that time, there was only

a pump. Water from it ran down the sink pipe, through a hole in the outside wall of the house, into a long wooden trough, and out of the trough into the ground in the field back of the house. Cicily-Ann thought this was the most interesting thing on the farm. For hours, Aunt Martha said, she would sit by that trough waiting for someone to use the pump, so that water would come out through the hole in the house. If it came spouting out in a stream, she watched fascinated. If it only trickled through, she put out her paw from time to time to catch a drop and examine it as if she were studying it carefully. Aunt Martha would pick her up and carry her to the barn or to one of the sheds where she was supposed to hunt mice. But even if Cicily-Ann was shut up in one of these places, she usually managed to escape and get back to her watching post. At last Aunt Martha gave up. "You're only an old sinkspout watcher!" she told Cicily-Ann. And Uncle Sven got another cat.

The pump and the trough had long since been replaced by more modern plumbing, but Cicily-Ann Sinkspout still kept her funny last name.

"Nancy! Nancy!" called Aunt Martha.

Nancy jumped; she must have dropped off to sleep thinking about Cicily-Ann. She got up quickly and put on her pretty red-and-green-plaid jumper and the white blouse which Mamma had embroidered in red. By the time she had run downstairs Whoa-Emma was coming up the driveway.

What a jumping and hugging and squealing! One would have thought that Nancy had not seen Grandma and Aunt Anna and the girls for months! First Grandma had to admire all the flowers Nancy had arranged. Then the children disappeared to carry out their important part of the secret and didn't show up again until Aunt Martha called them to dinner.

The field where Uncle Sven would be working that afternoon was near the birch grove so he could come to join them for coffee about three o'clock. Uncle John, who did not have to work Saturday afternoons, would come, too; but Grandpa could not be there because Saturday was his busiest day.

After dinner Uncle Sven carried to the grove a chair for Grandma and two blankets for the rest of the party to sit on. Aunt Martha and Aunt Anna divided all the other things into seven bundles so that each guest should have something to carry and nobody have too much.

"I guess the house can take care of itself this

afternoon," said Aunt Martha. "Danny can come, too."

And off they all went, eight birch gatherers, counting Danny.

"There will be ten at the party," said Elsa, "when Uncle Sven and Papa get there."

"Ten?" said Aunt Anna. "Look behind you."

The children turned and saw, following them through the field, Cuckoo Clock and, farther behind, Mrs. Hooligan, Aunt Martha's pet hen. Mrs. Hooligan had been a weak little chicken, and Aunt Martha had taken her into the kitchen and nursed her back to health, so that she had become a real pet and expected special privileges.

Nancy laughed. "You never know what's going to happen on this farm," she said. "May they come with us, Aunt Martha?"

"Oh, sure," said Aunt Martha, "as long as it's so near home. Mrs. Hooligan can go back to the barnyard if she gets tired of us, and Cuckoo Clock follows you around everywhere anyway."

As soon as they reached the grove and put down their bundles, Grandma took charge.

"Now, children," she said, "I will show you what to do. We must remember to be very careful not to harm any of the trees or the little bushes that are springing up around them. Take only

branches that are so crowded they cannot grow well. We must never forget that God gives us all good things to use and to enjoy but never to waste. Pick branches like this. See it is thicker than a broomstraw but not too thick."

"Why don't the grownups cut the branches," suggested Aunt Martha, winking at the girls, "and the children take off the leaves?"

"Yes, that will be good," said Grandma, "and then we can peel the twigs later."

"May we take the branches over there near the edge of the grove in the sun?" asked Sigrid, winking back at Aunt Martha.

"Yes, as soon as we have some ready for you. Carry one of the blankets over there so you can sit on it while you work."

As soon as a few branches had been cut, the children began their work. Elsa and Helga picked off the leaves as fast as they could, being sure that the stem was left on each. Nancy and Sigrid fastened the leaves together carefully and evenly, but they also had to work quickly. They planned to make a wreath for Grandma's hair, and if there was time, they would make also a garland to put around her neck. But all this they must do without Grandma's seeing them. They sat with their backs to her, and luckily she was so busy that she did not come to see what they were doing. Every now and then when they laughed aloud, she looked over in their direction and smiled, but that was all. As long as children were busy and happy Grandma let them alone.

"It's good that Aunt Martha gave us these darning needles to make the holes in the leaves," whispered Sigrid to Nancy. "The stems are so soft they wouldn't do it, but once you get a couple of holes in a leaf, it's easy to weave the stem of another one through."

"Yes it is," Nancy whispered back. "Aunt Martha said we should stick some leaves in slantwise like this so the wreath will be wider, and put some leaves on top of others so it won't be too thin."

From time to time Helga ran to get more branches. It didn't take so long to cut off leaves as it did to fasten them together, so Elsa and Helga began to work on the garland. "Make that the thickness of one leaf," Sigrid whispered. "It won't take so long."

"Let's sing," said Aunt Anna, and she and Grandma and Aunt Martha began to sing the Swedish songs Grandma and her friends had sung when they went gathering birches in Sweden long ago. Songs of birds and flowers and the out-of-doors they were; and there in the spring-green woods, the New England birches now heard the songs their sister birches in another country had heard each spring for many, many years.

"Now you sing, children," said Grandma, and the little girls sang the songs they were learning for the Decoration Day exercises they would soon have in school. American songs this time. "We're tenting tonight on the old campground"; "Mine eyes have seen the glory of the coming of the Lord"; "Just before the battle, Mother." It must be admitted that they had no very clear idea what these were all about, but they loved to sing them anyway.

"Don't begin 'My country, 'tis of thee,' " said Nancy, "because we can't stand up right now."

"Your turn," said Sigrid to the grownups. And so it went; and whether the songs were Swedish or American it didn't matter—they all made the spring afternoon lovelier. When the singing was over, Nancy looked up at the trees.

"This is a green and white day," she said. "See the white of the birches and the green leaves and the green grass and the white flowers on those bushes over there."

"Your name is green with a little gold in it, Nancy," said Elsa.

"Yours is white with a little blue," said Nancy, "and Helga is blue and Sigrid is rose."

"There you go with your colors again!" said Sigrid.

Nancy and Elsa had discovered that they saw words and names in color and were never tired of comparing notes. Sigrid and Helga did not have this gift and could not understand what the other two meant.

"How can you *tell* what color a name is?" Sigrid said. "You're just making it up."

"No, we're not, honest," said Elsa. "Nancy is as misty green and gold as anything; and Sigrid is rose. To me the name Helga seems yellow, though."

"It does?" said Nancy. "Oh, no, it's blue as blue."

"What color is Cuckoo Clock?" asked Elsa.

"Blue-gray," said Nancy.

"No, more brownish," said Elsa, "and Danny is green and Hooligan is red and yellow."

"Oh, you're crazy," said Sigrid.

And just then Aunt Anna called, "How are you coming along, girls?"

"Fine," said Sigrid. And indeed they were; they had a garland long enough to go around Grandma's neck and reach down to her waist, and a wreath, too. "Is it most time for the party?"

"Yes," said Grandma. "John will soon be here and you have been good children. Let us now spread the tablecloth."

"There comes Papa!" cried Helga and ran out into the field to meet him. Elsa went to tell Uncle Sven coffee would soon be ready. Aunt Anna unwrapped the blanket that was keeping the coffeepot hot, and the others unwrapped coffee bread and cookies, sugar, cream, and milk. They were careful to keep the birthday cake hidden from Grandma.

"Let's scatter the birch leaves we didn't use on the tablecloth," said Sigrid. "The green on white will look pretty."

Uncle Sven and Uncle John came; Grandma's chair was drawn up to the "head of the table" and then the little girls brought the first surprise. Singing "Happy Birthday to You," they came up to Grandma's chair. Sigrid and Nancy carried the wreath and placed it on her lovely white hair. Elsa and Helga put the garland round her neck.

Grandma was so surprised she could hardly speak. She tried to gather all four children into her arms at once. "Thank you, dear, dear children," she said. "To think you were making these beautiful things and I did not know it at all." She touched the garland lovingly; she lifted her hands and felt the wreath on her head. "You make me feel like a queen."

"You are a queen," said Nancy. "You are Queen of the Birch Festival."

"You look beautiful, Grandma," said Helga.

"Yes, she does," said Aunt Anna, "but we don't want the Queen's coffee to get cold. Get your other surprise, children."

"Another surprise!" said Grandma. She had not noticed that Aunt Martha and Uncle John were busy lighting the candles on the cake. Now it was ready and the four little girls all helped to carry it. They had frosted it with pink and white and the candles were pink. Aunt Martha had baked the cake in a sponge-cake pan, so it was shaped like a ring. In the center the children had placed a small glass of water and put into it the apple blossoms Nancy had saved. The glass did not show but the flowers did, as if they were growing right out of the cake. Grandma couldn't get over how lovely it was.

"Come on, everybody," said Aunt Martha. "I'm going to pour the coffee."

"And I will pour the milk for the children," said Aunt Anna.

Even after they had finished eating, they did not want to leave, but sat there in the late afternoon sunshine.

"Was it like this in Sweden, Grandma?" asked Nancy.

"Yes, something like it," said Grandma, "but our birch grove was on a rocky hillside and from it we could see our little red farmhouse. And my mother used to bring us coffee. And I was young then and after we had gathered the birch twigs, we used to play games down in the field below, and sing and dance about. It used to be so good to have spring again after the long, cold winter. And a Swedish spring—oh, a Swedish spring!" But she could find no words to describe the springtime of her childhood.

"Why did you leave Sweden when you loved it so much?" asked Sigrid.

"Like many other people I left because it seemed that things would be better for us in this new country. We could buy more land or get work in the cities that would pay us enough to give our children many things we had not been able to afford."

"Did you ever go back?" asked Nancy.

"No, Grandpa and I could not afford to," said Grandma. "It takes much money to sail across the ocean, and even here in America we had hard times often—sickness and trouble—but always we worked, Grandpa and I, and it has been good. Yes, it has been good."

"Do you love Sweden more than you do America?" asked Sigrid.

"No," said Grandma, "but the country where you were a child, that country you never forget. It seems to me that the grass was greener and the birches whiter, and all the flowers brighter-colored than they are here. But that is most likely only because I am looking at them through the eyes of memory."

"I don't see," said Nancy, "how any place could be lovelier than this farm."

Grandma smiled at her. "Wait till you are as old as I am. It will seem even lovelier to you, thinking of it then, than it does now, and you will understand what I say today. No birches will ever look so white to you; no apple blossoms will ever smell so sweet."

"Anyway, you aren't sorry you came to America, are you, Grandma?" asked Elsa, putting her head down on Grandma's knee.

Grandma looked around at them all.

"No, I am not sorry," she said. "This is a good, good land. Here Grandpa and I found each other;

here we had our sons and daughters, and now there are our grandchildren. No, I am not sorry I came. I would do it all over again."

They were silent for a little while until Aunt Anna said, "Sing, John."

"Oh, yes, please, Papa, sing," said Sigrid.

Uncle John had a beautiful voice and they all loved to hear him sing.

"What will you have?" he asked.

" 'Sköna Maj, välkommen,' " said Sigrid.

"It seems a little late to welcome May," her father laughed, "but if that's what you want, all right."

So he sang that, and other songs, too, and the others sat and listened.

"Somebody else's turn now," he said at last.

"I know," said Helga, "now we can stand up, so we could sing, 'My country, 'tis of thee.' " And they stood up and sang the song that told how much they all loved America.

> "I love thy rocks and rills,
>   Thy woods and templed hills . . ."

they sang, and Nancy realized that she had never really thought before today what those words meant. They meant the brook with the rocks in

it where she and the Carlson girls would play in
the summer, and the birch woods where they
stood now, and the hills they could see in the distance. She sang with all her heart.

"Now, since it is Grandma's birthday, let us
sing her song all together," said Uncle John.

Nancy knew that song. It was about the prov-
ince in Sweden where Grandma had lived, beautiful Vermland. Once when Nancy and her mother
and father had been visiting at Grandma's, Uncle
John had sung for them about beautiful Vermland. Nancy's father had said it was one of the
loveliest songs he had ever heard—that anybody
hearing it, whether he had ever seen Vermland
or not, would feel the love of Vermland in his
heart. It was true. Nancy could feel it now as they
stood around Grandma singing her song. When
it was over, she thanked them again and again.

And still they were reluctant to leave this birch
tree party.

"Let us have just one more song," said Uncle
John, "and Nancy shall choose this time. She is
the only one who hasn't asked for something.
What shall it be, Nancy?"

"Could we please have '*Sköna Maj, välkommen*' again?" asked Nancy.

"Oh, yes," said Sigrid, "and all sing it this time.

142

Nancy knows it, too, Papa. Grandpa has taught it all to her, hasn't he, Nancy?"

"Yes, he has," said Nancy. "We have sung it every day this whole month."

"Good for you," said Uncle John. "And do you know what the words mean?"

"Well, just about, I do," said Nancy. "They mean beautiful May is our friend and is welcome to our village again. When I wrote to tell Mamma what song we were learning, I asked Grandpa if it was all right to call it 'Lovely Maytime, welcome to our hearts and homes again.' He said I had the right idea."

"And so you have," said Uncle John, "and I wish Grandpa were here to sing it with us."

They all wished that and thought of Grandpa especially as they sang the May song. When they had finished, little Helga threw her arms around Grandma's waist.

"Well, I'm glad, anyway," she said, "that you came to America, Grandma."

"Are you, my darling?" said Grandma, hugging her. "And why are you glad, I wonder."

"Because you love us all so much," said Helga instantly.

They all smiled at this, but years later, after Nancy was grown up, she realized how much

Grandma's love for them all and their love for each other had contributed to the happiness of that afternoon, although nobody but Helga had said anything about it.

It was an afternoon that Nancy never forgot. She could not, later, recall just how Grandma had peeled the birch twigs and made them into the little egg beater whisk brooms, but the birch-gathering party stayed in her memory forever. She could close her eyes and see again the white tablecloth spread on the ground, with the birch leaves scattered on it, and the sunlight making patterns as it shone through the trees above. She could see Grandma with her snow-white hair and the crown and garland of birch leaves; and the grownups and children sitting on the ground around her. Danny lying peacefully at Uncle Sven's feet; Cuckoo Clock in Aunt Martha's lap; Mrs. Hooligan scratching in the grass nearby. All of them—grownups, children, and animals—secure in the feeling that here they would never know anything but love and kindness. She could hear the faint tinkle of the cowbells in the distance and the happy Swedish voices singing, "Lovely Maytime, welcome to our hearts and homes again."

Chapter 8

"THE FUNNIEST CLUB IN
THE WORLD"

NANCY's third special day came at the end of a
week when everything had gone wrong. She got
up feeling so happy Monday morning, for this
was the week when Papa was coming to see her.
To be sure, he would not arrive before Saturday,
but she and Grandma had many preparations to
make for his visit.

Then, at noon, the postman brought a letter.
Papa could not come! He was, he wrote, as disappointed as she would be; but he knew that she
would understand. One of the men who worked
in the same store as he did had broken his leg, so
that the store could not spare Papa. Two men

away from work would be too much. This man and the one who owned the store had been very kind to Papa since Mamma had been sick and had allowed him to be away from work two days to take her on the train to the hospital, another two days to visit her, and had now intended to let him be away a busy Saturday and Monday so that he could see Nancy. Not everyone, Papa said, would have been so kind and considerate, and he could not desert these friends now in their trouble. Grandpa had written to tell him what a good girl Nancy had been, brave and cheerful; and he was proud of her. Now he would have to ask her to be still braver, and he knew she would be, and he would come as soon as he possibly could.

But Nancy was so disappointed there was no comforting her. Grandma and Grandpa felt as sorry as she did; and the Carlson girls, when they heard the news, were full of sympathy. They all tried to think of things to help Nancy bear her trouble, but it seemed that nothing did any good. "I just want Papa," she kept saying. Nobody blamed her in the least for being so sad, but Grandma and Grandpa began to worry about her.

"It can't go on like this, Nancy," said Grandma at dinnertime on Tuesday. "You have eaten hardly anything since you got Papa's letter and you must eat." But Nancy wasn't hungry.

"Would you like to come riding on the grocery wagon with Karl the Twelfth and me this afternoon?" asked Grandpa. But Nancy shook her head, although ordinarily she would have accepted this invitation with pleasure.

"Maybe the girls will be able to comfort you when they come after school today," he said hopefully. He had hardly finished speaking when there was a knock at the door. A boy who lived near the Carlsons had brought a note. All three girls had colds and Aunt Anna did not dare to let them come out this afternoon. By Thursday they would surely be all right and would come to see Nancy then. The boy also had a little basket of surprises the girls had sent her, but she wasn't really interested.

Grandma tried to get her to go out-of-doors, where June was making all the gardens on the street lovelier and lovelier. Nancy went, but only as far as the piazza, where she sat with her arm around Oscar, who snuggled up to her as if he, too, were trying to comfort her.

On Wednesday things were no better.

"Nancy," Grandma said, "you must get over this. You must try to remember how much better off you are than many people. Mamma is doing so well in the hospital, and you have a kind Papa who will come to see you as soon as he can. Think of Aunt Kristina's children. They don't have any Papa at all now and Henry doesn't even remember him, he was so small when his Papa died. Think how much worse that is."

"Yes," said Nancy, but she didn't really think anything was so bad as not having her father come to see her. All Monday afternoon and Tuesday she had felt sad; now she began to feel abused.

"It's not fair," she said to Grandma, "it's not fair for that man to break his leg just now when Papa was coming!" She knew that was an absurd thing to say, but she couldn't help it.

Grandma cooked the things Nancy liked best; the Carlson girls sent her their library books to read; Grandpa brought her a bag of candy and tried to amuse her by singing and by telling stories; but Nancy couldn't shake off the feeling that everything was wrong.

By Thursday morning she was not only feeling abused; she was downright cross. Nothing Grandma said or did was right! Now Grandma was more worried than ever. Nancy was an unusually good-tempered little girl. Ever since she had come in April she had been sunny and helpful and a joy to have around. It was so surprising to have her cross that Grandma was sure she must be sick.

"I think we ought to take her to the doctor," she told Grandpa when he came home to dinner. "I feel so worried I don't know what to do. It is worse than if she were one of our own; it is harder to take responsibility for somebody else's child. You aren't sure you're doing what they would want you to do."

Grandpa understood. "Wait and see what Anna says this afternoon," he said at last. "I don't know what a doctor could do, but if you and Anna decide it is best, we'll take Nancy to the doctor tonight. It's Thursday, so his office will be open."

But when Aunt Anna came, she was puzzled, too.

"It doesn't seem to be a case for a doctor," she said. "If only something would happen to shake Nancy out of it, she'd probably be all right. Still, I know how you feel. Before you decide, let's see what the girls' coming will do. Maybe they'll shake her out of it."

They did; but in a way nobody could have expected.

About four o'clock they came running into the yard, and it was plain that they were so full of excitement that they couldn't come fast enough.

149

"Nancy, Nancy," Sigrid called, "oh, Nancy! Elsa has a name day for you."

This really woke Nancy out of her spell. "How? What?" she asked eagerly.

"It's the most wonderful thing," said Helga. "Tell, Elsa."

"Well," said Elsa, "this afternoon Teacher told us a story and it gave me the idea. It was about Robert Louis Stevenson—you know, that wrote *A Child's Garden of Verses*—well, he heard about a little boy who was born on February 29 in leap year and so he had a birthday only once in four years. And Robert Louis Stevenson felt so bad for the little boy that he gave him, *gave* him his very own birthday so that he could have one every year. And if it's all right to give away a birthday, it must be all right to give away a name day. And, Nancy, I'm going to give you mine! Right now! You can have it for always!"

Elsa's eyes were shining and Sigrid and Helga looked at her with pride.

Grandma and Aunt Anna looked at Nancy. She had begun to cry.

"I don't want it," she sobbed. "It wouldn't be my own name. I—don't want it!"

Sigrid was disgusted. "You make me sick, Nancy Bruce," she said. "Here Elsa has done such a wonderful and generous thing and you don't even say thank you. You make me tired!"

"Well, I don't care," said Nancy, stamping her foot. "I don't want any name day but my own name day, and I should think you'd know that by this time. I don't care what that old Robert Louis Stevenson did. And it isn't fair! Everybody in this whole world but me has a name day. And it isn't fair!" And she began to sob hysterically.

"NANCY!" said Grandma so sharply that Nancy stopped crying out of sheer surprise; she had never heard Grandma speak crossly. The other little girls stood and stared in amazement at this sudden turn of events.

"I'm ashamed of you, Nancy," Grandma continued, "to act like this when Elsa has been so generous. We all can understand that you don't want any name day but your own, but to treat Elsa so! Go right upstairs to your room. Now! At once!"

Nancy went.

"You run outdoors and play, girls," said Aunt Anna. "I want to talk to Grandma."

They went out, but not to play—they were too stunned. Elsa's lovely plan had come to nothing; their usually sunny Nancy was in disgrace; and Grandma, *Grandma* had spoken so sharply they didn't know what to make of it.

"Well, I guess that's done it," said Aunt Anna. "Now she's had this flare-up she'll probably be all right."

"Yes," said Grandma a little doubtfully. "Yes, she'll probably be so sorry for what she did that I'll be able to do something with her now. This has probably been coming on all week, but I hope it's over."

Up in her room Nancy was sitting in her little rocking chair, so shocked at what had happened that she didn't know what she was going to do.

Grandma had spoken crossly to her; and Elsa— Elsa would probably never speak to her again. What would she ever do without Elsa? And Helga and Sigrid? They wouldn't want to play with her any more. What had come over her to make her act as she did?

When Grandma came upstairs after Aunt Anna and the girls had gone, and took her in her arms, Nancy cried again, but now she was calmer.

They did not go to the doctor that evening. Instead Grandpa hitched Karl the Twelfth to the buggy and they drove down to Aunt Anna's so that Nancy could tell the girls how sorry she was. "For it is not a good thing," said Grandma, "to go to bed when there are hard feelings between friends."

To Nancy's relief the girls seemed now to understand and were willing to play with her again, and she was able to make Elsa realize how much she appreciated her generous offer.

"I'll never, never forget how good you were, Elsa," Nancy said.

"You must all three come and spend all day Saturday with Nancy," said Grandma.

But first there was Friday, and that was one of the days Nancy would always remember.

After breakfast Grandma had a plan for her.

"I want to talk to you, Nancy," she said. "I am afraid this name day business is too much on your mind. It's too bad you don't have a name day, but if nothing anyone thinks of satisfies you, then you'll have to get along without one. You have spent all this week thinking of your own troubles. Here it is Friday and you have wasted almost a week of this beautiful month of June. Now, there is no cure for trouble like doing something for somebody who is worse off than you are. And that is what you are going to do today."

Nancy looked puzzled. "But I don't know anybody that's worse off than I am to do anything for."

"Well, no doubt there is somebody," said Grandma, "and you're going out to find that person. I want you to do just what I say. Put on your sweater and then go out and walk down the street as far as School Street and then cross over and walk up the street as far as East Street. If by that time you haven't found anybody that's worse off than you are, come home and we'll try again. But look everywhere."

"And what shall I do if I find somebody?"

"That's up to you. Run along now and look hard."

This was all extremely puzzling. Still, it was something to do, and Nancy started out. But how would she know if anybody was worse off than she was? How could she tell?

At the house next to Grandma's Mrs. Clark was working in her garden.

"Hello, Nancy," she called. "Isn't it a lovely June morning?"

"Hello," said Nancy. "Yes, it is. Your garden looks pretty," she added shyly.

"Yes, doesn't it?" said Mrs. Clark. "I love June—it's the most beautiful time of year, I think."

She sounded happy, not a bit worse off. Nancy went on.

On the piazza of the next house sat Grandpa Kramer sunning himself. Of course he was old and it was better to be young, but he didn't look sad. He looked happy.

"Isn't this a fine day, Nancy?" he asked. "What are you doing so early in the morning?"

"I'm—I'm taking a walk," said Nancy.

She couldn't very well say, "I'm out looking for somebody worse off than I am." Or could she? It sounded silly.

I'm out looking for somebody worse off than I am.

It sounded like a story. Once there was a princess and she was so . . . Nancy blushed and felt uncomfortable, for there was no doubt about the rest of the sentence . . . she was so cross that her grandmother said, "You must go out and find somebody worse off than you are." In a story, of course, the princess would find a beggar or a little match girl or somebody like that.

Nancy set off at a brisker pace. She looked in every yard all the way down the street and up the other side. There were neither beggars nor match girls on Grandma's street this morning. She saw a man delivering laundry. He was whistling. She stopped to pet two kittens playing on a lawn; nobody could be happier than they seemed to be. She saw a woman hanging out clothes; the woman waved gaily to Nancy. Everybody and everything looked happy this June morning. She had got almost up to East Street before she noticed the roses.

If she had not stopped to look at them, she would not have seen the person who sat on the piazza behind them. They were climbing roses, and they covered almost all the front of the piazza and part of one side. There must have been hundreds of blossoms, and they were the freshest and gayest little red roses Nancy had ever seen. All the time she had been in the house feeling sad and cross, these beautiful roses had been growing outside. She stood on the sidewalk and looked and looked at them.

It was then that she heard a slight noise behind them and, stepping back a little, saw the boy. He was white and thin and he was in a wheel chair and there was a blanket over his knees. It must be that he couldn't walk at all. He couldn't walk this lovely June morning. He was worse off than she was. She had found someone! But now that it had happened she didn't know what to do. She just stood there, and then suddenly she turned and ran home to Grandma. Or almost home. When she got into the yard, she began to go more slowly. Somehow it seemed that she hadn't acted the way a person should when she found somebody worse off than she was herself. Grandma was on the piazza.

"Well," she said, "how did you get on?"

"I found somebody," said Nancy slowly, "a boy in a wheel chair. He was sitting on a piazza behind the most beautiful climbing roses I ever saw."

"And what did you do about it?"

"Nothing," said Nancy sadly. "I didn't know what to do. I couldn't think of anything to say to him."

"You could have said hello, couldn't you?" said Grandma.

"Yes, I could have done that, but if he said just hello, what could I have said next?"

She began to feel miserable. She knew that Sigrid and Elsa and Helga would have found plenty to say; they wouldn't have run away.

"I could go back and try again," she said.

"Good," said Grandma.

"He'll think I'm funny to come back," said Nancy.

"Oh, no, you can tell him the roses are so pretty you wanted to see them again."

"Would a boy want to talk about roses?" asked Nancy doubtfully.

"Well, my goodness, you don't need to keep

on talking about roses," said Grandma. "Say that to get started."

"All right," said Nancy and went up the street again.

This time the boy had moved out from behind the roses. He was sitting in the sunlight reading a book. He looked up when Nancy came, but he didn't say anything.

"Hello," she said bravely, "your roses are so pretty that I wanted to see them again."

"They're crimson ramblers," he said. Then his face began to grow crimson; he turned quickly away from Nancy and appeared to be absorbed in his book.

And that seemed to be the end of that. Nancy went sadly home. On the way she thought of any number of things she could have said, but it was too late now. All she could do was go back and report to Grandma.

"You *are* having a hard time," said Grandma. "I tell you what—Oscar has got back from his calling. He has gone into the barn to rest, but I'm sure he'll be glad to start out again. Take him along and see what happens."

"That boy will surely think I'm a funny girl," said Nancy.

"Now who is it you're thinking of?"

"Oh," said Nancy, "all right. I'll try once more."

This time things went better. As soon as they came near the crimson rambler house, Oscar dashed ahead of her and up on the piazza.

"Hi, Rover!" said the boy, petting him. And then to Nancy, "Is this your dog?"

"No," said Nancy, "he's my grandfather's, and his name isn't Rover. It's Oscar."

"*Oscar!*" said the boy. "Is this Oscar? Is your grandfather the man that has Karl the Twelfth?"

"Yes," said Nancy. "Do you know Karl the Twelfth?"

"Yes, I used to feed him sugar every day. And your grandfather told me about Oscar."

"Oh, my goodness," said Nancy, "you must be Alex."

"I am, but how did you know my name?"

"Grandpa told me about you and how you fed Karl the Twelfth when he delivered groceries next door to your house. But I thought that was in another part of town."

"It was. We moved here this week. Does Karl the Twelfth live near here?"

"A little way down the street. He's a nice horse, isn't he?"

"He's wonderful," said the boy almost fiercely.

"He's about my best friend and I was afraid I wouldn't see him any more. Will he come up this way?"

"Sure," said Nancy. "I'll tell Grandpa. He'll bring him."

And now instead of not being able to think of anything to say, she couldn't talk fast enough. She talked about Karl the Twelfth and about Oscar and Teddy. She talked about all the animals at the farm. She told how she happened to be with the Bensons and not in school. She told about the Carlson girls and said she would bring them to see him. She told about name days; Alex had never heard of them, but he was interested.

"Do I have one?" he asked.

"I don't know. Do you have a middle name? Because if there isn't a name day for Alex, maybe there'd be one for your middle name, anyway."

"It's Arthur. Alexander Arthur Brown."

"I'll look as soon as I go home," said Nancy.

"Don't go yet," said Alex. "Tell more about the animals."

The front door opened and a pleasant lady came out carrying a tray with three glasses of milk and a plate of cookies. "It's morning lunch time," she said.

Nancy was embarrassed. "I think I'd better go

home. I—I came for a walk and I saw the roses," she explained, "and so I came again." It wasn't quite all the truth, but she was sure it wouldn't be right to say she had come to look for somebody worse off than she was.

"Oh, don't go," said the lady. "I am Alex's mother, Mrs. Brown, and you must be one of our neighbors."

"She's Nancy," said Alex, "and she's visiting Karl the Twelfth and this is Oscar. They live almost across the street. She's going to have Karl the Twelfth come to see me."

"Then you must surely stay," said Mrs. Brown, "because Karl the Twelfth is one of our best friends. How nice that he is a neighbor, too! And I'm glad you like the roses. They are crimson ramblers and I never saw any so lovely."

"I never did either," said Nancy, "or so crimson."

"Or so rambly," said Alex, and they all laughed and had their party.

"I'm certainly glad that I came on this walk," said Nancy. "I've had such a good time. I think I'll go exploring often. Say, Alex, why can't we go together? Your wheel chair will go on the sidewalk, won't it? We could go walking every morning, up the street and down the street, and have adventures. We could go exploring. It could be like a club, you know. We could be an exploring club."

Alex seemed doubtful.

"I can't see that there'd be many adventures on this street," he said.

"Well," said Nancy triumphantly, "that's what I would have thought yesterday, but look what happened. I call having found you an adventure, and your knowing Karl the Twelfth and everything. And besides, I saw the ramblers. We could find something new to see every morning, and it would be more fun if there were two of us."

Mrs. Brown interrupted her.

"I think it would be a wonderful idea," she said. "I'm sure you'd have some adventures. At least you could call on all the animals on the street, Alex. You'd like that."

"Oh, yes," said Nancy. "I saw two lovely kittens this morning and I know one lady that has a parrot and another that has a canary. Oh, there'd be lots to see, all right. Why, often Grandpa and I go in the buggy with Karl the Twelfth along some country road, just rambling along, and we find all sorts of interesting things."

"Rambling along with Karl the Twelfth would be quite different," said Alex. "I'd rather go

164

rambling along with Karl the Twelfth than do anything else in the world."

"You would?" Nancy said. "Well, then you can."

"I *can?*" said Alex.

"Sure," said Nancy, "there's plenty of room in the buggy seat for three and Oscar will sit on the floor. He always goes, too."

"Oh, may I, Mamma?" Alex asked eagerly.

"I don't know," said his mother. "I'm afraid it might be too much trouble for Mr. Benson."

"Oh, no it wouldn't." Nancy was sure of her ground here. "Grandpa loves children and he'll be glad to have Alex go. And the buggy will be as comfortable as the wheel chair and Karl the Twelfth never gets excited the way Whoa-Emma does. He just goes rambling along."

"I guess we should call our club the Ramblers," said Alex, laughing.

"Yes," agreed Nancy, "because some days we can ramble up and down this street and some days we can ramble in the country with Grandpa. You know what we should call it? We should call it the Crimson Ramblers! Because if it hadn't been for them, I might not have seen you; and we can have a crimson rambler rose for our emblem!"

"The Crimson Ramblers," said Alex, as if trying the name out. "Yes, it sounds all right unless you know it's a rose; then it seems kind of sissy."

"Why, Alexander Brown!" said his mother. "What do you mean—sissy? Hasn't all the reading we've done together made any impression? Don't you remember the Wars of the Roses? There was nothing sissy about those."

"The Wars of the *Roses!*" said Nancy, enchanted. "What were they? Do you mean somebody fought wars with roses?"

"No, of course not," said Alex a little scornfully. "There were two royal houses in England, and they each had a rose for an emblem—the red rose of Lancaster and the white rose of York."

"How wonderful!" said Nancy. "Are there any stories about them?"

"Yes," said Mrs. Brown, "and some rainy days when you can't ramble, I'll read some to you and Alex. Would you like that?"

"I'd like it more than anything," said Nancy. "I'd love to hear more about the Wars of the Roses. All I could think of when you said that was a war where people threw roses at each other! It would have been a pretty war," she added.

Mrs. Brown laughed. "Oh, Nancy, you're a darling," she said, "and you've done us more good than you'll ever know."

"*I* have?" Nancy said in surprise. "I haven't done anything; I've only had a good time."

Suddenly Alex began to laugh. "I—I—I got to thinking," he said finally, "that this must be the funniest club in the whole world." He began to laugh again. "Five members—one man, one girl, one boy, one horse, one dog!"

"It's going to be a *good* club," said Nancy.

"You bet!" said Alex.

And it was. Grandpa went right over to the Browns' that noon as soon as Nancy had told him how much Alex wanted to ride with Karl the Twelfth. While he was gone Nancy hunted for Alexander and Arthur in the Almanac. They were both there.

"Well, I call that the limit," she said to Grandma. "Alex isn't any more Swedish than I am. And both his names are in the Almanac and not one of mine!" But just now she was too happy to worry, even about name days.

When Grandpa came back, he had things all arranged. There was no time like the present, he said. He had to deliver groceries out in the country that afternoon, and as none of the packages was heavy he could easily take the children, too, and they could have their first Crimson Rambler ride that very day.

He came for the children about three o'clock. "I'm not much of a joiner," he said to Mrs. Brown, "but this strikes me as a good club to belong to."

Then Mrs. Brown did a thoughtful thing. She got her camera and took a picture for Nancy to send to her mother. She made the members stand in a row. First came Karl the Twelfth with a bunch of crimson roses behind his ear; then Grandpa and Alex with roses in their buttonholes; then Oscar sitting up straight and important with a spray of roses dangling from his collar; then Nancy with roses twined in her hair.

Nancy was thrilled. "This is a wonderful, wonderful day," she said. "And I've learned three things already. I've learned that if you want to have adventures, you just have to go out to look for them."

She stopped, thinking what an exciting morning it had been.

"And what are the other two things you learned?" asked Mrs. Brown.

"Oh," said Nancy, "I learned about the Wars of the Roses and I learned that if you want to get acquainted with a boy, always take a dog along."

Grandpa lifted Alex carefully into the wagon and made him comfortable; then he and Nancy

and Oscar got in; and Karl the Twelfth rambled off.

The first meeting of the Crimson Ramblers was a complete success, and when Grandpa and Nancy got home, they couldn't say enough good things about Alex.

"He's the nicest boy, Grandma," said Nancy. "He's so *funny*."

"Yes, he's a fine boy," said Grandpa. "I can't get over that I never gave him a ride before when he wanted one so much. But I never realized. His mother seems to be able to give him everything he wants; they must be very well off and I never thought he'd care to go riding in an old wagon. It never dawned on me to ask. Poor little fellow; he'll never be able to walk, his mother told me; but he'll make his mark in the world anyway, that one. He's a smart boy and so interested in everything. I'm proud to know him."

"Me, too," said Nancy. "And wasn't it lucky I foun . . . *Grandma!* Did you know all the time that he was there?"

"Yes," said Grandma, "Grandpa told me last night that he had heard they had moved into the house where the Carters used to live."

"Then," said Nancy, "why didn't you tell me

to go right up there instead of having me go down one side of the street and up the other?"

"I thought it might be more interesting that way," said Grandma.

Nancy thought a moment. "Well, it was," she said. "Much."

Chapter 9

ANOTHER NEW FRIEND

THE June days grew lovelier and lovelier as Nancy and Alex rambled up and down the street to see what they could see. Oscar was a busy dog now, for he not only had to do all his regular calling; he felt that it was necessary for him to join the children in their expeditions, too. He was a faithful Rambler.

They had promised that they would not try by themselves to get Alex's wheel chair over the curbstones; so one day they would explore one side of the street; the next day Mrs. Brown would take the chair across the road and they would do their exploring on the other side. In this way they could stop at Grandma's house for their morning lunch when they were on her side and at Mrs. Brown's when they were on the other. They had thought they might extend their journeys around the block, but they could never find the time to do so. There was so much to see right on their own street! It took a whole morning for one side.

There was Grandpa Kramer, who always had time to tell them a story of his own childhood and to hear of their adventures of the previous day. There was Mrs. Donovan, who had lived in Ireland and was so jolly that she always had some little surprise for them when they came to call on her—something from Ireland to show them; a sample of something she was cooking for them to taste; a funny story to tell; or a song that they could learn. There was old Mr. Jensen, who had lived in Hans Christian Andersen's country and once, as a little boy, had been taken to see the Round Tower. Alex and Nancy knew about this Tower because of the story, "The Tinder Box." It was thrilling to know, too, somebody on their street who had seen this famous place.

They stopped to play with the two kittens, Muff and Puff. Oscar always looked bored during this performance, but he was too good-natured even to tease a kitten and lay and rested beside

Alex's chair. They called on the canary and if he happened to be in a singing mood, stopped to listen to his song. They talked to the babies. They spoke to all the grownups, and every one had something pleasant and friendly to say.

There was the parrot. Grandma said it would be all right to ask Mrs. Lindstrom, who owned him, if she would show him to Alex. One day Nancy went up the Lindstroms' front steps and rang the doorbell. Mrs. Lindstrom was glad to bring the parrot's cage out where Alex could see it. The parrot could say several words, some in Swedish, some in English. "Pretty Poll! Pretty Poll!" he could say. "Polly wants a cracker. Polly wants a cracker." And in Swedish: *"God dag! God dag!"* This meant "Good day! Good day!" But it was pronounced so that it sounded like "Good dog! Good dog!" and Oscar always thought the parrot was saying it to him.

One morning Mrs. Lindstrom showed the children Poll's funniest trick. She let him out of his cage. Then she got her carpet sweeper and began to run it over the hall carpet. Poll flew over and perched on the sweeper. "Hurry up! Hurry up!" he cried. Up and down the hall he rode. If Mrs. Lindstrom slackened her pace at all, Poll cried, "Hurry up!" The children thought it was the funniest trick they had ever seen. After that, each time they came down Mrs. Lindstrom's side of the street, she kindly showed them the trick again. "I have never had such a clean hall carpet as I have this spring," she said.

Nancy had never thought much about this street. On it there lived grownups, high school boys and girls, and babies; until Alex came there had not been any children of her own age to play with. Now she found everything on the street interesting.

The places Alex enjoyed most were Grandpa Kramer's because he told such good stories, and Grandma Benson's. Oscar favored Mrs. Lindstrom's because he could never get enough of hearing Poll say, "Good dog! Good dog!" One of Nancy's favorite places was Mrs. Hackett's, for in her yard there was a budded rosebush that would soon be covered with little yellow roses. It was the only yellow rosebush on the street. Sometimes, even when Alex wasn't with her, Nancy ran over to see how the buds were coming along. Mrs. Hackett was happy to have her do this, because she loved the rosebush more than anything else in her garden.

"My grandmother brought it over from England," she said.

"You mean this very rosebush used to grow in England?" Nancy asked.

"Yes," said Mrs. Hackett, "why, have you ever been in England?"

"Oh, no," said Nancy, "but just about my most favorite book is about a little girl in England." She told Mrs. Hackett about Griselda and the cuckoo. "And maybe this rosebush grew right near Griselda's home," she finished.

"Maybe it did," said Mrs. Hackett.

Nancy couldn't get over the wonder of it.

Now when the Carlson girls came to Grandma's, they always went to call on Alex, too. "Don't stay too long," Grandma would say. "Too many of you will make him tired." But Alex seemed to grow stronger every day. Mrs. Brown said that she had never seen him so happy.

Something else happened that gave all the children pleasure. Nancy's father sent her a riddle book. The girls had often asked each other the few riddles they knew; they had never imagined there could be a whole book of them. But here they were—*one hundred and one riddles*! Now the girls and Alex took turns asking the riddles from the book. Alex and Nancy asked their friends on the street, and some of them remembered riddles from their childhood which weren't even in the book! "The world seems to be full of riddles," said Nancy.

Two of the riddles became the children's favorites. One was easy; yet nobody could guess it. "What makes a coach dog spotted?" Everybody tried, thinking there was some special reason why that special kind of dog should be spotted. Everybody had to give up. "What makes a coach dog spotted?" "His spots." The children never tired of this.

Their other favorite was a hard one. They did not even know what it meant and still they loved it. Sigrid came upon it first when it was her turn to ask the riddles:

"Why is a pig with a curly continuation like the ghost of Hamlet's father?"

They stared at her in astonishment.

"What's that curly-con-thing you said?" asked Helga.

"And who is Hamlet and what does it *mean*?" asked Nancy.

"I don't know," said Sigrid, "but isn't it *funny*?"

They agreed that it was.

"What's the answer?" asked Alex

Sigrid read it. "Because he could a tail (tale) unfold."

"A tail, tale!" said Helga. "What's a tail, tale?"

They could hardly stop laughing. It didn't matter that they didn't know what the riddle was all about; it became part of their conversation.

"Hi, Alex," Nancy would call when she came running over in the morning with some special news for Alex, "come on out, I can a tail, tale unfold."

And if they were all sitting together talking, Alex might say to Elsa, "Why don't you unfold a tail, tale for us?"

If they heard a noise they couldn't account for, or if a door slammed suddenly, one of them was sure to say, "Must be the ghost of Hamlet's father."

Mrs. Brown could have told them all about Hamlet and explained the riddle to them; but they never asked her or anyone else about it. It was their secret riddle.

"Next Hallowe'en," said Sigrid, "I'm going to ask Mamma for an old sheet and I'm going to be the ghost of Hamlet's father."

"I'll be a tail, tale," said Helga. "Old Tail, Tale," Alex used to call her after that.

Everything about that riddle struck them funny.

181

"It was worth the price of the book," Sigrid said years later when they were all grown up and talking over old times.

"It must have been the funniest introduction anybody ever had to Shakespeare," said Elsa.

On the days Grandpa had to go to the country to deliver groceries he now arranged things so that all five Ramblers could go. One Sunday he invited Alex, Nancy, Oscar, and the Carlson girls to go for a ride in the two-seated carryall, and the five original members voted to make Sigrid, Elsa, and Helga Ramblers, too.

"Good," said Nancy, "now it is even—four ladies in this Crimson Rambler Club and four gentlemen."

Toward the end of June, Alex and his mother went to spend a week with his grandmother. Nancy expected to be lonesome; she did not know what an exciting thing would happen while he was gone.

During that week came the Day of Yellow Flowers.

It began with such a lovely morning that Nancy got up even earlier than usual and ran across the street to Mrs. Hackett's garden. Mrs. Hackett was there ahead of her with gardening shears in her hand.

"Aren't the roses beautiful, Nancy?" she said. "I'm cutting a little bunch of them for you to put in your room with the yellow-rose paper."

Nancy was delighted. She carried the roses home carefully. They were little and sweet, and as yellow as buttercups. Grandma gave her a glass, and she arranged the flowers and put them on the little table in her room. Right after breakfast she had to run upstairs to look at them again. Yellow roses on the wallpaper and yellow roses on the table. It was perfect.

Then she heard Aunt Martha's voice in the kitchen. She must have come in unusually early this morning with her eggs.

She had, and for a special reason.

"Nancy," she said, "you remember I told you that the little schoolhouse at the foot of the hill near the farm is fifty years old this year? Well, the children are planning to have a celebration on the last day of school, and they want to decorate their classroom as it has never been decorated before. They plan to make it a regular bower of daisies. They were going to do it tomorrow, but last night Miss Lane, their teacher, told me that Mr. Smith, who owns the farm next to the school, said the children would have to get all the daisies picked this morning. He's got to begin mowing the hay in the field where they grow first thing this afternoon. The children will be ready to go out about ten o'clock, and I said I thought you'd be glad to help. They will need all the willing hands they can get. Do you want to come to the farm with me now and stay through tomorrow night so that you can go to the last-day exercises with me?''

Nancy was thrilled. Grandma hurried to help her pack the things she would need. "You sit down, Martha," Grandma said, "and drink a cup of coffee and eat a piece of my fresh coffee bread while we get Nancy ready."

In no time at all Aunt Martha, Nancy, and Whoa-Emma were on the way to the farm. Nancy had been so excited about the sudden plan that she had forgotten to pack her library book; she had forgotten her pencils and crayons; she had even forgotten Charlotte and Jasmine. But she had not forgotten the yellow roses; she held them in her hand.

"I am going to put them in my room at the farm, Aunt Martha," she said, "and then I'm going to put the Griselda book on the table right beside them, because maybe their rosebush grew right in the garden where Griselda used to play."

Whoa-Emma was in high spirits and went

along at such a rate that they were at the farm at half-past nine.

"Nancy," Aunt Martha said, "even before I unharness Whoa-Emma I'm going to show you something. Shut your eyes and let me lead you around to the north side of the house. Don't open them until I say you may."

Nancy was mystified, but she did as Aunt Martha had ordered.

"Now stand still, and when I say three, open your eyes. One—two—three!"

Nancy's eyes flew open.

"O-o-o-h!" was all she could say.

While she was at the farm in May this field in front of her had been a field of green. Now it was a sea of daisies and buttercups—white daisies with glowing yellow centers; and, growing here and there among them, the most golden buttercups in all the world.

"Oh, Aunt Martha!" she said at last. "Aren't they *lovely*? So *yellow* and so *white*! May I walk out into the field?"

"Yes, while I put Whoa-Emma in the barn. But come right back; we must go down to the school as soon as we can."

So, still holding the little bunch of fragrant yellow roses, Nancy walked down among the

white and yellow daisies and the golden buttercups.

"Mayflowers and apple blossoms and lilacs;
crimson ramblers and yellow roses; daisies and
buttercups," she said to herself. "Are spring and
summer always like this up here, I wonder?"

To the end of the daisy field she walked, making a little path that closed behind her as soon as
she had passed. The sky was blue; the maples near
the pasture fence were in their fullest green; along
the stone wall by the road the wild roses were
coming into blossom; bees flew in and out of the
white and rosy clover flowers in the field nearby.
But now Nancy saw only the daisies and buttercups; she could not take her eyes off their dazzling
summer loveliness.

Finally Aunt Martha had to call her, and Danny
came running to get her.

"But I'll come back," she said to herself, "I'll
come back to spend the whole afternoon in the
daisy field."

It was a happy morning. Miss Lane and the
children were working in the schoolhouse when
Aunt Martha and Nancy arrived. They had
scrubbed the classroom so that everything shone,
and now they were glad to rest long enough to eat
the cookies Aunt Martha had brought them. She

had made them last night especially for this treat, and they were not dainty afternoon-party cookies. They were large and round and thick, rich with eggs and cream, and sprinkled with sugar. One was enough for Nancy, but the big boys who had been up and working since four o'clock ate six or seven apiece!

Then they all went out into the field back of the schoolhouse. Some of the boys had filled big washtubs with water and set them in the school shed. The children were going to put the daisies in these to keep them fresh until the next morning when they would decorate their schoolroom. Nancy was invited to come to help, and she was delighted to accept the invitation. Nothing like this had ever happened in her city school; she had never seen a room that was a bower of daisies.

For two hours they worked as hard as they could. At the end of that time every tub was full of daisies. They made the old shed look like a beautiful place.

Nancy and Aunt Martha went home to dinner. After they had eaten, Nancy had to lie down for an hour. She was really tired after her busy morning, and she fell asleep and did not waken until three o'clock. She would be losing the afternoon if she didn't hurry.

She went outdoors and wandered through the daisies. She sat under the biggest maple tree and looked at the field. She climbed up on the stone wall and looked at it from there. Any way you looked at it, it was a wonder!

She decided she would get her library book and read it under the maple tree. Then she remembered that she had not brought the book with her. Of course she could get *The Cuckoo Clock*, but since the day she had first read it near the colored glass window, she had not wanted to read it anywhere else for fear of breaking the spell.

Suddenly she had an idea. She went back to the house and found Aunt Martha in the kitchen.

"Aunt Martha," she said, "you know the old box up in the attic where *The Cuckoo Clock* was? Can I go up and see if there is anything else in it I want to read?"

"Why, yes, you may if you want to, but I can't believe that there will be. I feel sure you and the girls would have found it already if there had been."

"I think I'll look anyway," said Nancy.

She went up into the attic. Over in a corner was the old box. Nancy opened it; it certainly didn't look promising. The papers in it were

brown with age, and the books did not look at all like children's books. Most of them were Town Reports, whatever they might be. She had almost given up, when at the bottom of the box she saw a much smaller book. Its covers had been torn off, or perhaps worn off with age. She could not tell what the name of the book was, but when she opened it, she saw that it contained poems. They were not children's poems, but at least they looked more hopeful than Town Reports. She let her eyes wander over the pages, and stopped to read a few lines here and there. Some of them she did not understand at all. Some were wonderful.

> "The splendour falls on castle walls
>   And snowy summits old in story,"

Nancy read; and

> "The year's at the spring,
>   The day's at the morn,"

and

> "Under the greenwood tree
>   Who loves to lie with me . . ."

She turned to the first poem in the book. It began:

"Spring, the sweet spring, is the year's
pleasant king."

She read the first two stanzas. When she came
to the third, her eyes widened in surprise:

"The fields breathe sweet and daisies
kiss our feet."

"Well, my goodness!" said Nancy aloud. "It's
even about daisies!"

She put the Town Reports and the papers back
in the box; took the little book and went downstairs. Aunt Martha was in the vegetable garden
now. Nancy waved to her and went back to the
daisy field. For an hour she sat under the old
maple tree with the book. It was different from
any she had ever had—hard in some places but
good to read in others. Alone there among the
daisies Nancy read aloud the poem about them.
She read parts of other poems, too; but she kept
coming back to

"The fields breathe sweet and daisies
kiss our feet."

She was glad she had found the book. She
wished she knew what the name of it was, though.
At first she thought there was no clue to that
name anywhere, but then she noticed that the

first two leaves of the book were stuck together. Maybe if she could get them apart, she would find the name. She hunted until she found a thin, sharp little stick; then carefully she began to pry the leaves apart. She worked until she could make out the words on the almost hidden page.

"*The Golden Treasury of Songs and Lyrics,*" Nancy read slowly. Her eyes shone. She did not know what lyrics were; she did not even know what an important day this was for her; she did not realize that on this lovely summer afternoon she had discovered poetry. She only knew that she had found a book she wanted to keep and to share with Elsa.

"A *golden* treasury," she said to herself, "in a field of golden flowers."

It was then that she saw a little girl coming up the road.

She was a jolly-looking little girl with long flaxen braids. She wore a rather faded pink dress and carried a basket on her arm.

"Who can she be?" Nancy wondered. She was not one of the school children, but she must live nearby. She couldn't have come from far away, dressed only in a play dress.

The little girl came over to the stone wall and began to climb up on it. She was coming into the field! She stepped down among the flowers. "And daisies kiss her feet," thought Nancy.

The little girl now walked slowly—slowly through the daisies. As she came nearer Nancy saw that the basket she was carrying on her arm was not at all the kind of basket one would expect to see a little barefoot girl in a faded pink play dress carry in a daisy field on a summer afternoon. It was not a basket for flowers or for berrypicking. It looked more like a sewing basket, and it had a cover and a handle. It had flowers painted on one side of it. It looked as if it belonged in a parlor or a little girl's bedroom. "What can be in it?" Nancy wondered.

But she could not have guessed. It would have been harder to guess the answer to that question than to any of the riddles in her riddle book. If she had had one hundred and one guesses, she could not have guessed what was in that basket.

Chapter 10

THE VIOLET BASKET

THE longer Nancy looked at the basket, the more fascinated she became. She was looking at it so hard that she was actually startled when the little girl said shyly, "Hello."

Nancy jumped. "Hello," she said, "oh, hello."

"The lady in the farmhouse told me to come up here to play with you," said the little girl doubtfully, as if she were not sure of her welcome.

This brought Nancy to her senses. "Oh, I'm so glad you've come," she said. "Do you live near here?"

"I'm going to. We're moving into the house

across the road from your farm. The lady saw me in the yard and came across and asked my mother if I could come over to play with you. So I came."

"Well, I *am* glad," said Nancy so enthusiastically that now there was no doubt in the little girl's mind that she was welcome. "Aunt Martha told me that somebody was going to move into the Collins place, and I hoped and hoped there'd be some children. My name's Nancy. What's yours?"

"Wanda," said the little girl.

"*Wanda!*" said Nancy. "Is it *really*? That's my middle name and my favorite name in the whole world and I never knew anybody else of that name. My mother got it out of a book. Why, it practically makes us twins or something, doesn't it? How old are you?"

"Nine," said Wanda.

"So am I. Then we are almost twins. My birthday is January 25. When's yours?"

"February 14," said Wanda.

"February 14! Valentine's Day. Aren't you lucky! To be a Valentine and have the name Wanda. I love that name."

"I don't like it very well. I'd much rather have Nancy."

196

"You *would*! Oh, no! Wanda's much prettier. I wish people would call me Wanda."

"I will if you want me to," said Wanda.

"Oh, will you?" said Nancy. "And I'll call you Nancy," she said with sudden inspiration, and both little girls burst out laughing.

"Hi, Wanda!" said Wanda.

"Hi, Nancy!" said Nancy. "We'll get everybody all mixed up. Won't it be fun? Have you got any brothers and sisters, Nancy?"

"No sisters, Wanda," said Wanda, "only brothers, and they're all older than I am. Seven brothers," she added in a disgusted voice, "and not one sister."

"I don't even have any brothers," said Nancy.

In the excitement of learning her new friend's name, Nancy had forgotten the basket, but now she noticed it lying on the ground close to where Wanda had sat down.

"What a lovely basket," said Nancy. "I was so surprised to see you come walking through the daisies. And the basket was another surprise. I mean, well, I mean it isn't the kind of basket you'd—well, it isn't a berrying basket or anything."

"It's a sewing basket," Wanda said. "My godmother gave it to me and I love it more than anything and I didn't want to put it in the moving wagon so I carried it out to our new house myself. And now everybody's putting things down every old place; and boys aren't ever careful. And I— well, I was afraid somebody might break it or something, so I didn't dare to put it down," she finished.

"I don't blame you a bit," Nancy said. "I wouldn't have left it either. It's so beautiful. I never saw a basket with a bunch of flowers painted on the outside of it before. Could I see inside it?"

"Oh, yes," said Wanda, so eager to show off the lovely basket that her excited fingers fumbled with the catch that opened it. "My godmother bought the basket and then the lady she works for gave her the most beautiful piece of silk, to match the violets on the outside, to line the basket. There! See!"

"O-o-o-h!" said Nancy in admiration. The silk had a creamy white background that was sprinkled with little clusters of purple violets with tiny yellow centers and green leaves.

"Violets are my favorite flower," said Wanda.

"Yellow roses are mine," said Nancy, "but this basket is perfectly beautiful. It is the most beautiful basket I ever saw."

"Smell it!" said Wanda, holding it up to Nancy's nose.

"Why, it smells like perfumery!" said Nancy.

"Sachet!" announced Wanda proudly. "My godmother put sachet powder under the lining to make it special."

"It's wonderful. And look at the darling little pockets around the side! May I see what's in them?"

Wanda pulled each lovely article out in turn, beaming with pleasure at Nancy's appreciation. In one pocket was a tiny pair of scissors, in another a little thimble. In one was a box with tiny spools of thread of different colors. There was a needlebook with covers made from the violet-sprigged silk, and cream-colored flannel pages buttonhole stitched around the edges in violet and crimson and rose. At the bottom of the basket was a card decorated with gold. On the card was some writing that Nancy could not read.

"What does it say on the card?" she asked. "It isn't English, is it?"

"No," said Wanda, "it's Polish," and she lifted the card and began to translate its message to Nancy. Slowly she read:

"With congratulations and best wishes to my dear little goddaughter Wanda on her name day."

"Her WHAT?" Nancy cried, jumping up so quickly that *The Golden Treasury* landed on the ground. She stooped to pick it up, but her eyes did not leave Wanda's now bewildered face. "Her WHAT?"

"My name day," said Wanda, looking at Nancy. "My name day. A name day is . . ."

"Oh, I know what a name day is," Nancy interrupted. "I know what a name day is all right, but there isn't a name day for Wanda."

"There is, too!" said Wanda. "What do you mean?"

"Well, it's not in the Almanac."

"Almanac?" said Wanda. "I don't know what you're talking about."

"I'm talking about name days," said Nancy, "and there isn't any for Wanda or, anyway—. Quick! Let's go look. Quick. Hurry!"

To Wanda's increasing mystification, Nancy pulled her to her feet. "Come on, let's go down to the house—*quick*!"

Nancy was off through the daisy field with a thoroughly bewildered Wanda following after.

"Aunt Martha, Aunt Martha!" Nancy called, long before they had reached the house, and there was such urgency in her voice that Aunt Martha

came hurrying to the door that looked out onto the field.

"What's the matter, Nancy?" she asked. "Are you hurt?"

"No, but there's a name day for Wanda and I have to see the Almanac Book *quick*!"

"Well, my goodness," said Aunt Martha, "you almost scared the life out of me and it looks as if you'd scared Wanda, too. The Almanac won't run away. Calm down a little and tell me what this is all about."

"It was in the basket, the violet basket," said Nancy.

"What was in the basket?" asked Aunt Martha.

"The name day for Wanda," said Nancy.

At this surprising statement Aunt Martha looked as much bewildered as Wanda. But now Nancy was in the kitchen with the Almanac in her hand.

"What day is Wanda Day?" she asked

"April 17," said Wanda.

Nancy turned to the April page and ran her finger down the dates. The name for April 17 was not Wanda. It was Elias. She almost cried at this new disappointment.

"No, it isn't Wanda," she said. "It isn't. I should have known it wouldn't be."

"It is, too," said Wanda. "It is. It is! We always celebrate Wanda Day on April 17. And I know some other Wandas and they do, too."

"Wait a minute!" said Aunt Martha. "Calm down, both of you, and tell me the whole story."

"I was sitting in the field," said Nancy, "when Wanda came, and I watched her coming and she had a lovely basket on her arm and it looked almost like a magic basket or something and then she showed me inside it. It's beautiful, Aunt Martha, and there's a card in it. It's written in Polish, but Wanda knows what it means in English. Read it, Wanda."

So Wanda read the card again:

"With congratulations and best wishes to my dear little goddaughter Wanda on her name day."

"Nancy," said Aunt Martha, "I guess you have your name day all right. Here is something we never thought of. We looked only in the Swedish Almanac. Because our American friends never celebrate name days, I guess we thought only Swedish people did. How foolish we were! Do Polish people celebrate their name days, too, Wanda?"

"Yes, they do."

"It seems," said Aunt Martha to Nancy, "that although you're a little American girl you have

one Polish name and you had a name day for that
all the time and we didn't know it. But I think
we'd better tell Wanda what this is all about."

She turned to Wanda and explained about
Swedish name days and how much Nancy had
wanted one and how they had all tried so hard to
find one for her.

"And now you have done it, Wanda," she said.
"And I think she deserves one of our great big
cookies, don't you, Nancy?"

"Yes, she does," said Nancy, "and I deserve
one, too, to celebrate."

"And I deserve one, too," said Aunt Martha,
"after working so hard to get head and tail to
what you were talking about. Get them for us,
please, will you, Nancy, and I'll open a bottle of
raspberry drink so it will be a real party."

They took their cookies and drinks out on the
porch.

"Isn't it wonderful!" said Nancy. "I've got a
name day at last. Aunt Martha! Maybe Nancy is
a Polish name, too."

"I doubt it very much indeed," said Aunt
Martha, "but remember you said you'd be satisfied with a Wanda Day because you love that
name so much."

"I am satisfied. I'm so happy. There's only one

thing—I can't help wishing Wanda Day came in the summer so that I could have a name day party while I'm at Grandma's. Now I have to wait until next year, and I may not even be here then."

Aunt Martha was about to answer when they heard Whoa-Emma coming up the hill.

"I didn't know Uncle Sven had gone to town," said Nancy.

"Stand up and see if you can see if anybody is riding with him," said Aunt Martha.

Nancy stood up. There in the wagon were Sigrid, Elsa, and Helga!

"My goodness, are they coming out for supper?" asked Nancy.

"They have come to stay through tomorrow night," said Aunt Martha, "as a special surprise, so that they can help at the school here and go to the last-day exercises."

"But tomorrow is a school day in their own school," said Nancy.

"I know, but I thought that for once in their lives they should be excused for such an important reason as a fiftieth-anniversary celebration here, and since school in town is so nearly over and all three girls have been doing good work, I stopped in to see Aunt Anna this morning before I came to get you. I had quite a time to persuade her that this was important, but she finally agreed to ask the girls' teachers if they could be excused for a whole day. And evidently they could!"

What excitement when Whoa-Emma stopped at the kitchen door and the little girls came jumping out of the wagon! They had to explain that they had been as much surprised as Nancy was.

"To be excused for a whole day!" said Sigrid. "And not because we are sick or anything. Isn't it wonderful? I didn't know such things ever happened."

"Oh, anything can happen in this world, just anything. That's why life is so exciting," said Elsa, dancing up and down.

"Nancy will tell you that is surely true," said Aunt Martha, and then she introduced Wanda to them all.

"And I've got a Wanda Day!" said Nancy.

"WHAT?" cried all three little Carlson girls at once.

"It's the most exciting thing," said Nancy. "I was sitting in the field and a little girl came and I thought daisies kiss her feet and then I saw the basket and it was Wanda and it was in it—in a violet basket only it was in Polish and her godmother gave it to her . . ."

She stopped, suddenly conscious of the puzzled way the Carlson girls were looking at her.

"For mercy sake, what *are* you talking about?" asked Sigrid. "Godmothers and daisies and violets! And what basket and what was in Polish? What a tail, tale!"

Aunt Martha burst out laughing. "You certainly got that mixed up, Nancy," she said. "Try again and begin at the beginning."

"But I did begin at the beginning," said Nancy. "Wanda did come through the—oh, you tell, Aunt Martha!"

So Aunt Martha told.

Sigrid and Elsa and Helga were almost as pleased as Nancy herself. They had to examine and admire the wonderful basket, and marvel at the fact that Wanda had come through the field carrying it and Nancy had been unable to keep her eyes off it.

"And I never dreamed," said Nancy, "that in the bottom of it was my name day."

"Isn't it *romantic*," said Elsa, "to have a name day come in a violet basket!"

They had been talking so excitedly that they had not heard the boy who now came up on the piazza. It was one of Wanda's brothers. "Mamma wants you to come home now," he said.

Aunt Martha welcomed him as a new neighbor, and then he and Wanda said goodbye.

"I will come over later this evening, Wanda," said Aunt Martha, "and explain to your mother about what's going on at school tomorrow, and maybe she'll let you come, too."

It was after Wanda had gone that Elsa made a wonderful suggestion.

"Aunt Martha," she said suddenly, "Nancy didn't have a chance to celebrate her name day this year, so couldn't we do it as soon as school closes? It could be a name day party for Nancy Wanda and a welcome party for the new Wanda. Wouldn't it be all right, Nancy, even if it is late, so long as you really have a name day now?"

"Oh, yes!" said Nancy.

"That's a fine idea," said Aunt Martha. "We'll speak to Grandma before we decide definitely, but I'm pretty sure she'll agree."

"Nancy hasn't celebrated her name day in any of her nine years," said Sigrid, "although she has had one every year."

"Then we'll have to make this nine times as nice as an ordinary name day would be," said Elsa decidedly. "A nine-times-nicer name day!"

"In all my life," said Nancy, "I have never had such an exciting day as today."

"Can we have it like in a fairy tale, Aunt Martha," asked Elsa, "with feasting that lasts for seven days and seven nights?"

"Nine days and nine nights, it should be," said Helga.

"No, you can't, monkeys! One day is quite enough, but we'll make it a very special one. Come now and help me get supper. You must go to bed early because you'll be up later than usual tomorrow night."

It was lucky they could all work and talk at the same time; otherwise Uncle Sven would have found no supper when he came in that night. Even at bedtime Aunt Martha had difficulty in quieting her excited little guests.

"Girls," she said finally, "if you don't settle down to go to sleep, you'll all be too tired and Grandma and Anna will have a right to blame me for interfering with your regular school day and they won't want to let you come out here again."

"We'll go to sleep right off," said Sigrid instantly. "You don't know how wonderful we think you are to plan this treat for us. We'll quiet down this minute, won't we, girls?"

They all agreed, and even before Aunt Martha had got back to the kitchen three little girls were fast asleep.

But Nancy was still awake. She couldn't keep this exciting day from whirling round and round in her head. It didn't seem possible that it was only this morning that Mrs. Hackett had given her the yellow roses and Aunt Martha had come for her and they had gathered daisies at the school. And then there had been the old poetry book. In all the excitement Nancy had forgotten to show it to Elsa, but she would, and together they would read it.

> "Spring, the sweet Spring, is the year's
>   pleasant king;
> Then blooms each thing . . ."

Nancy began to think about the spring. To Sigrid and Elsa and Helga, who had spent so much time in the country and so often watched the gardens around their home and school blossoming, there had been nothing unusual about this year. They had taken it for granted. But to Nancy this spring had been like a picture book unfolding. She could see many of the pictures now.

There were the mayflowers peeping up from the dead leaves the day they found Cuckoo Clock; there were the hepaticas and anemones they had found on a Saturday walk in the wood near

Grandma's house; there were the pansies and tulips and flowering shrubs coming into blossom in her garden. There was apple blossom week at the farm with the wonderful night in the orchard. There were the crimson ramblers behind which she had found Alex; and Mrs. Hackett's yellow rosebush. And now the golden field of daisies and buttercups and Wanda coming with her violet basket.

"I am really going to have a name day party," Nancy thought, "and I have had a spring of flowers."

And then four little girls were fast asleep.

Chapter 11

PLANS AND SECRETS

It was amazing how much talking was necessary to plan a name day party. As soon as the little girls were awake in the morning, they began to chatter so that Aunt Martha came to the foot of the stairs and told them she thought there was a flock of magpies in the attic.

"Get up, magpies," she said, "it's almost time to go to the school." The children scrambled into their clothes, talking all the while, and hurried down to breakfast.

"You know what I think," said Elsa. "I think we should keep the party a secret from Wanda. It seems to me a welcome party ought to be a surprise. Don't you think so, Aunt Martha?"

"Yes, I think you're right," said Aunt Martha, "but that means you can't talk about it at all today because she'll be with you. And that's just as well, because you want to keep your minds on helping the school children; and besides you mustn't plan too much before you are sure Grandma is willing for Nancy to have this Wanda Day party."

The little girls weren't worried about Grandma. "She'll love it," said Sigrid. "She'll help us make it a nine-times-nicer name day. But we won't say a word about it to Wanda. Oh, won't it be exciting to surprise her!"

"Here she comes!" called Aunt Martha. "Good morning, Wanda. Don't you look nice and fresh in your pretty plaid dress. You'd better start now, girls. Tell Miss Lane that I'll be along about ten o'clock with a little lunch for you all."

It was a lovely, sunny morning.

" 'What is so rare as a day in June?
    Then if ever come perfect days,' "

said Elsa. "That's out of a poem the seventh grade is learning. I heard some of the kids saying it. And this is a perfect day—daisies and buttercups and wild roses, and all of us having a holiday. Let's run!"

The Carlson girls knew Miss Lane and some of the children, but it wouldn't have mattered if they hadn't known any of them—Sigrid, Elsa, and Helga all had the happy gift of making friends instantly and were at home anywhere. They introduced Wanda and soon all the children were busy.

The big boys were putting up nails and hooks to hold the daisy chains that were to be hung from each corner of the room to the other diagonally opposite. Where these two chains crossed there was to be a star made of buttercups, like a star in the sky, over the heads of the people who came to the exercises. Miss Lane had cut out a cardboard star and made many small holes in it so that buttercups could be stuck in to cover it entirely.

Across the back wall of the stage the boys had stretched a piece of chicken-yard wire, and the bigger girls were now putting green branches into the holes in the wire, with bunches of daisies here and there among the leaves.

The Carlson girls and Nancy and Wanda sat out on the lawn with one group of school children and made daisy chains as fast as they could. They could hear the brook that ran back of the schoolhouse and the faint sound of cowbells in the distance. The smell of new-mown hay was so sweet that they had to take long breaths of it every now and then.

"What a wonderful place to go to school!" said Nancy.

"Every day isn't as exciting as this," said one of her new friends. "It's good you all came to help. We can make the room even prettier than we could have if we'd had to do it all alone."

By the time Aunt Martha came with a basket of fresh gingerbread squares, the room had already begun to look like a bower of daisies. By noon, when the children went home, Nancy thought she had never seen such a beautiful place. There were festoons of daisies over the windows and the doors; there were bouquets of daisies on Miss Lane's desk and on the organ. There were stone crocks with daisies and green branches in them on the stage, where the children were to sing and to speak their pieces. The chicken-yard wire didn't show at all now; it seemed to be a green wall with daisies growing out of it. The daisy chains had been hung from corner to corner under the ceiling, but the buttercup star was to be kept in a cool place until the last minute, so that it would look fresh and beautiful in the evening.

"I never saw such a lovely room," said Sigrid.

"It is lovely, isn't it?" said Miss Lane. "Thank you all for coming to help."

"We loved it," said Sigrid.

"Although we didn't know you very well before," said one of the schoolgirls, "now it seems as if we were all friends."

"We are," said Elsa. "With daisy chains we are bound together in eternal friendship! We'll see you all tonight."

Wanda had been invited to stay to dinner at Aunt Martha's; so there could be no talk of the name day party. But there were plenty of other things to talk about, and the afternoon seemed short. The children had all brought their best white dresses, and after an early supper they got ready for the evening.

"You look like a bunch of daisies yourselves," said Uncle Sven.

"Why don't you each put a few daisies in your hair?" suggested Aunt Martha.

The children were delighted and hurried to do so. Uncle Sven put a daisy in his buttonhole, and Aunt Martha tucked a few in her belt. Together they all walked to the school.

The buttercup star was now in its place and shone with beauty against the white daisies. The girls were surprised and pleased to find that the school children had reserved a whole front row for their willing helpers. It was fun to be there and to hear the singing and the recitations. It was fun to be part of the excitement that followed, when everyone talked and laughed and drank lemonade and ate homemade cake. It was sad to say goodbye to the daisy-bowered schoolroom, but it was wonderful to walk home in the starlight.

Helga was rather tired, so she walked between Uncle Sven and Aunt Martha, holding a hand of each. Sigrid and Wanda, who had found that they had many interests in common, walked ahead, talking all the way. Elsa and Nancy came last, their arms around each other. Now Nancy told Elsa about the poetry book and said the verse about the daisies.

"It's beautiful," said Elsa, "perfectly beautiful. We'll read the whole book this summer. How wonderful that you thought of looking in the box again."

They didn't say much more; it was good to walk quietly in the starlight, just being friends.

Early in the morning Aunt Martha took the girls to town, and after the Carlsons had been left at their house, she turned Whoa-Emma toward Grandma's.

"I can hardly wait to tell Grandma about Wanda Day," said Nancy.

"Don't you think it would be better if I told her?" said Aunt Martha. "You do get so excited and mixed up about it."

"All right," said Nancy, "but you'll tell her first thing, won't you, please?"

"I will."

When Grandma had heard the whole story she said that of course Nancy Wanda should have a nine-times-nicer name day. Nancy was so excited she couldn't stop talking long enough to let Grandma and Aunt Martha have their visit.

"You are getting yourself all worn out," said Grandma at last. "I think you'd better take Teddy and go upstairs and have a little nap. One of the first things you'll have to decide is who is to be invited to this party. Would you like to have the girls in Sigrid and Elsa's Sunday School class? They could come some Saturday afternoon. Or maybe there is somebody else you'd like to invite. You lie still and think about that until you fall asleep."

Nancy took Teddy and went upstairs. He curled up in the crook of her arm on the bed, and she lay patting him gently.

Then suddenly and surprisingly she felt frightened! She didn't really know the girls in the class with Sigrid and Elsa; and she did not have their gift of getting acquainted easily. A name day party had always sounded like so much fun—with the house all decorated, and Grandma playing the piano, and a crown and a cake, and everybody in Swedish costume. But what if the girls didn't like it and she couldn't think of anything to say? And she didn't have any Swedish costume; she was sure all the others did. She would be the only one without one. Teddy snuggled closer into her arms and she patted him again, but she was close to tears. Yesterday and this morning a Wanda Day had seemed the most wonderful thing in the world.

She looked around the room that she had grown to love so much. The yellow roses seemed gayer than ever. Grandma had put a small bunch of lavender heliotrope on the table to welcome her home. Several morning-glories that had not yet closed for the day peeped in at her window. Charlotte sat in her small rocking chair, and Nancy now saw that Grandma had washed and ironed her little forget-me-not-sprigged dress so that it looked as if it were new. Suddenly there was a noise on the stairs and Oscar came bounding up, licked Nancy's face in welcome, and then settled down on the bed with her and Teddy. Everybody was so good to her. It was, as Grandpa had said when she first came, like having a whole new family to love her. After she had made so much fuss about a name day, she couldn't tell them now that she was afraid.

And in the next minute she wasn't afraid at all! She knew exactly the kind of name day party she wanted. She knew what people she wanted to invite. A nine-times-nicer name day it certainly would be. Lying there thinking about it, she fell asleep.

She didn't wake up until Grandpa and Karl the Twelfth came home to dinner. Oscar had gone and Teddy was standing up giving himself a good stretch. She could hear Grandma telling Grandpa something in the kitchen, about the Wanda Day, probably. She got out of bed quickly, brushed her hair and ran downstairs.

"Here's my girl home again," said Grandpa, picking her up and kissing her. "Great things have been happening, I understand; and we'll have to call you Nancy Wanda now."

"Oh, yes, Grandpa, at least I've got a middle-name day. Isn't it exciting? And Grandma, I know just what kind of name day party I want."

"Tell us," said Grandma.

"Well, you know when we were out at the farm gathering the birches and Grandpa couldn't come, Uncle Sven said we'd all have to have a picnic out there soon. Could we make my name day cake at home some Saturday soon and then right after church on Sunday go out to the farm and have the party in the pine grove near the brook? And instead of having the girls in Sigrid and Elsa's Sunday School class, could I have just my own this-year family and my own dearest friends, both people and animals? You and Grandpa and Karl the Twelfth and Oscar and Teddy; and all the Carlsons and, of course, Wanda; and Alex and his mother; and Uncle Sven and Aunt Martha and *all* the animals at the farm? Oh, could I?"

Grandpa and Grandma laughed, and Grandpa said that sounded to him like the best possible kind of name day party. And it would certainly please Alex to see the farm and all the animals. Grandma thought the idea was good—with some slight changes.

"Oscar and Karl the Twelfth will be happy to come, I'm sure," she said. "But Teddy would just be unhappy. We'll have to leave his treat for him here at home and give him extra coffee in the morning and another snack when we get back at night. And then—have you thought about the name day cake? What kind of a pan would we have to get and how many barrels of flour for a cake big enough for all the people and two horses, two dogs, eight or nine cats, seventeen cows, five pigs, and a hundred or two hens?"

But Grandma's eyes were laughing and Nancy laughed, too.

"Well, maybe they won't all have to have cake," she said.

The first Sunday in July was set for the party, and grownups and children began to make plans. The men had to decide how to get everybody out to the farm; the ladies had to plan about the food and who was to make what. Suddenly everyone began to act mysteriously. "There are more secrets in the air than there are at Christmas time," said Grandpa.

Grandma and Nancy had to have a great many consultations about the name day cake. For her party Grandma had made a Swedish coffee cake; but she told Nancy she could choose any kind she wanted.

"I think I'll have chocolate," said Nancy. "I'll have a Polish name day and a Swedish party and an American cake. Will that be all right?"

Grandma said it would. "But you mustn't tell anybody but me anything about it," she added.

"You be thinking how you want to frost and decorate it."

Nancy had a different idea every day.

She had to spend a good deal of time with Sigrid and Elsa and Helga, for they were all planning surprises not only for Wanda but one for Alex, too.

One afternoon Nancy came running into the kitchen just as Aunt Anna was opening a package to show Grandma. Nancy was almost sure that must be a surprise, too, because Aunt Anna quickly laid a newspaper over the package and tried to pretend it wasn't there.

One day little Helga almost told a secret.

"We're going out to the farm all day the Saturday before the party," she began.

"Sh-h; sh-h!" said Sigrid and Elsa; and Helga put her hand over her mouth.

Sigrid began to talk about something else before Nancy could ask any questions; but she couldn't help wondering what they were going to do at the farm a whole day. She knew they would make her name day crown; but that wouldn't take all day Saturday. What could it be?

"Everybody seems to be planning a secret but you and Alex and his mother, Grandpa," Nancy said.

Grandpa didn't answer. Nancy looked at him. "Do you have a secret?" she asked.

"I might have a little one," he said.

Alex and his mother were much interested in the party; but they didn't act the least bit mysterious, so nobody guessed that they had a secret, too.

The Saturday before the party came—the day for making the name day cake. Now Nancy had decided exactly what she wanted, and early in the morning she and Grandma went to work. It was fun to mix and bake the cake and see it come out of the oven exactly as a proper cake should. It was even more fun to frost it.

Nancy took some of the powdered sugar Grandma gave her and mixed it with milk and a little vanilla until it was the right consistency. Then she spread it carefully over the top and sides of the cake. The top now looked like a large oblong piece of white paper on which it would be easy to write and draw. Then she made some more frosting, but this time she used egg yolks instead of milk; they made the frosting yellow. With this lovely color she made a border around the cake and wrote WANDA in large letters in the middle. Then she put some yellow flowers here and there.

"I don't know if anybody will guess that they

are yellow roses," she said doubtfully. "It's hard to draw with a stick dipped in frosting—much harder than to draw on paper with a pencil. But I can tell everybody what they are and they do look nice. Now for the violets for Wanda."

Grandma and Nancy had a hard time trying to figure out how they could make violet-colored frosting. Suddenly Grandma had an idea. She opened a can of last summer's blueberries. By mixing some of their juice with sugar Nancy was able to get frosting that made good violets, and these were much easier to draw than roses. At last the cake was done.

"Now," said Nancy, "everything is ready for the party."

Chapter 12

THE GOLDEN NAME DAY

"In all the time of all the world," said Elsa, "I don't believe there has ever been a lovelier Sunday than this one! Isn't it wonderful! I'm sure this will be a nine-times-nicer name day, Nancy."

Nancy was sure of it, too. She was sitting with Grandma and Elsa in the back seat of Grandpa's carryall. Grandpa, Mrs. Brown, Alex, and Oscar were in front. Alex was driving Karl the Twelfth. Uncle Sven and Aunt Martha had driven in to church in their two-seater, and now Uncle John, Aunt Anna, Sigrid, and Helga were riding with them, just ahead, in case Whoa-Emma took a notion to go like the wind.

"When we go up any hills," Uncle John had said as they were starting, "some of us will get out and walk so that we'll not tire the horses too much."

"The day even smells wonderful," said Nancy, as they came out into the open country.

"It's the hay in the fields," said Elsa. "I love it. When I grow up and use perfumery, I'm not going to have sweet pea or lily of the valley or anything; I'm going to have a special kind made for me called New-mown Hay."

"And whenever you come near us," said Mrs. Brown, smiling at her, "we'll think of Nancy Wanda's name day party."

The ride was lovely, but of course the party didn't really begin until they got to the farm. The minute they arrived Nancy had her first surprise.

"Come on upstairs quick, Nancy," said Elsa, as soon as they had reached the farmhouse door. "Quick! Never mind anything else. It's *important!*"

Nancy hurried after her. Sigrid and Helga were already in the front bedroom, and there on the bed were three—no, four!—Swedish costumes.

"It's yours, it's yours!" said Helga, dancing up and down in front of Nancy. "This one's yours.

Mamma and Aunt Martha made it for you. It's your name day present. Put it on."

"Mine!" said Nancy. "You mean it's really mine to *keep!* My very own?"

"It certainly is," said Sigrid.

And now Aunt Anna came to help the girls get dressed. She smiled at Nancy's pleasure in the costume and was glad to see that the little white blouse, the full, gathered red skirt, the gay striped apron, and the black velvet bodice all fitted. There were a pair of red socks and a little cap, too. As soon as she was ready, Nancy had to run down to show herself to Grandma and all the others.

"A real little Swedish name day girl," said Grandpa.

He had made Alex comfortable on the porch so that he could see what was going on while everybody was getting ready for the picnic and enjoy to the fullest the surprise the little girls had prepared for him.

But first they must go to get Wanda. Aunt Martha had explained everything to Wanda's mother, so she was all ready for the children when they came running over.

"Wanda, Wanda," she called, "come see who is here."

Wanda was in the kitchen, but she came running to the front of the house. The girls took hold of hands and began to dance around her.

"Surprise, surprise!" they cried.

Wanda was dressed in a lovely Polish costume even gayer than their Swedish ones.

"What is it? What *is* it, Mamma?" she asked. "Why have we all got on our costumes; why did you have me put on mine?"

"Go with the girls," was all Mamma would answer.

They ran across the road and now Nancy was as surprised as Wanda. In the driveway stood the old one-seated wagon Uncle Sven sometimes used when he went to town alone. But now it was almost entirely covered with daisies. Across the top of the seat had been fastened a large white paper on which Sigrid had printed with green crayon:

WELCOME TO THE TWO WANDAS

"We got the idea from the decorations at school," said Elsa, "and yesterday Mamma came out with us and she and Aunt Martha helped and we made this. It's a daisy chariot for you to ride to the grove in. Do you like it?"

Did they like it! No words could have said how

much they liked it or how proud they felt when Uncle Sven helped them into the seat and they sat in their name day chariot like two little princesses.

"This is a NINETY-times-nicer name day," said Nancy at last. "I never even imagined anything so wonderful."

"It is the loveliest flower cart I ever saw," said Grandma. "I don't see how you had time to finish it."

"We worked hard," said Sigrid. "But come on, girls, before we go to the woods, we have to you know what! Alex, shut your eyes for a little while until we say you can open them."

Wanda and Nancy got out of their chariot. Then as quietly as they could the girls picked up Cuckoo Clock and Cicily-Ann Sinkspout, who were on the steps, beckoned to Oscar and Danny, and disappeared into the house.

"Open your eyes," called Sigrid, "and wait to see what you will see."

Alex waited and waited and began to wonder if the girls were teasing him, but suddenly there was a sound of smothered giggles, of barking and the tramp of feet; and around from back of the barn came the funniest parade Alex had ever seen.

First came Grandpa leading Karl the Twelfth,

who was wearing a hat with daisies on it around the holes where his ears stuck through. Right up to Alex's chair they came, and Aunt Martha slipped something into his hand. It was a piece of loaf sugar. Alex, delighted, held it out to his friend. Karl the Twelfth took it and he and Grandpa marched on.

Next came Nancy leading a rather sheepish-looking Danny dressed in a paper hat with a poppy sticking out of the top. Aunt Martha handed a bone to Alex, and he gave it to Danny with a loving pat and words of praise. Next came Helga carrying Cuckoo Clock, who had a ribbon around her neck with a big bow that she didn't approve of at all. She didn't even wait for Alex to give her a treat; she yanked herself out of the bow and scrambled up on his shoulder and stayed there, as if she thought he would protect her from the foolish doings of little girls. Of course nothing could have pleased Alex more.

Cicily-Ann Sinkspout behaved better, stayed quietly in Sigrid's arms and daintily ate the piece of meat Alex held out to her. Meanwhile, Oscar, who was with Uncle John at the end of the parade, almost went wild with excitement and had to be let loose so that he could run up to Alex for his bone, way out of turn.

Aunt Anna carried Blacky, the Howling Success; Wanda, Grandma, and Mrs. Brown each had a cat or a kitten or two; Elsa had Mrs. Hooligan, and Uncle Sven brought Whoa-Emma. All the animals were decorated with hats or flowers or ribbon bows that the little girls had been working on for a week. All were glad to get a treat, but none took kindly to the idea of a parade.

"They wouldn't make very good soldiers," said Grandpa, but Alex thought they were all wonderful.

"It's a NINE-HUNDRED-times-nicer name day!" he said to Nancy. And he was delighted when Oscar and Danny came back to his chair to stay with him and Cuckoo Clock settled down in his lap.

In a little while everything was ready for the picnic. Wanda, Nancy Wanda, and Grandma got into the daisy chariot; Uncle John took one of the shafts, and Uncle Sven the other and acted as horses. Grandpa had lined a wheelbarrow with an old quilt. He now placed Alex in it and carefully wheeled him to the woods, stopping along the way to show him the hens, the pigs, the cow barn, and anything else he wanted to see. The Carlson girls ran along beside the chariot and the ladies followed behind.

"The other girls should have turns riding, too," said Wanda.

"Yes, they should," agreed Nancy.

"Later on," said Uncle John. "The two Wandas, I understand, are to ride now."

"Sing, Papa," said Sigrid, and Uncle John began an old Swedish song Nancy had not heard.

"It's about in the merry days of summer," Elsa told her.

"Well, this is certainly one of the merriest days I ever knew," said Mrs. Brown, when the song was done. "What a lovely song! Do please sing some more."

So they sang song after song, some in Swedish, some in English, until they came to the woods.

It was a real Swedish picnic meal that the ladies spread out; homemade rye bread and new butter; meatballs, sliced ham, and pickled herring; coffee and milk and almond-flavored coffee bread.

When all had eaten as much as they wanted of these good things, it was time for the name day cake. Everybody admired it when Grandma set it on the white tablecloth, and all knew at once that the flowers were roses and violets.

"Shut your eyes a minute," said Elsa to Nancy and Wanda. When they were allowed to open their eyes again, Elsa and Sigrid stood in front of them. Each held a crown of flowers. Nancy's was made of daisies and little bunches of yellow buttercups; Wanda's of daisies and tiny purple lady's-delight blossoms that looked like little, little pansies.

"It's too late for yellow roses and violets," said Elsa, "so we had to get the nearest things to them."

"They are lovely, girls!" said Mrs. Brown. "I don't see how you had time to do so many things."

"This is a NINE-THOUSAND-times-nicer name day!" said Nancy, as she and Wanda took off their costume caps, and Sigrid and Elsa put on the name day crowns. Then, together, Wanda and Nancy Wanda took hold of the knife Aunt Martha had brought and cut the roses-and-violets cake. Everybody had a good big piece, as well as a dish of homemade vanilla ice cream served right out of the freezer.

"When are we going to give Wanda her present?" asked Helga.

"Now," said Sigrid, and she ran to get two small boxes. She gave one of them to Wanda.

Wanda opened it. Inside was a tiny doll, like

the ones the other girls had. There was a card which read: "My name is Violet."

"She's from the four of us," said Elsa, "because we want you to have a flower-named doll, too. If you don't like the name Violet, you can change it. Any mother should have a right to name her own child."

"I like it to be Violet," said Wanda. "Thank you very much."

"Here's another box," said Sigrid.

This contained pieces of cloth and ribbon and a tiny card with the words: "For our new cousin, Violet, from Daisy, Marigold, Jasmine, and Trillium."

But even this wasn't the end of all the surprises. Mrs. Brown now had something to say.

"Alex and I have appreciated so much all that you have done to make us happy," she said, "that we wanted to do something to make Nancy and her little friends happy, too. So while we were away we bought a gift for Nancy and one for each of the Carlson girls. And then when we got home we heard about Wanda, and so of course we bought one here in town for her. And we hope you will like them."

She went to the chariot and out from under the

seat she took five strange-looking packages. They were all the same size and Nancy thought they looked as if they contained five sticks. What funny presents!

"Suppose you open them, one at a time," said Mrs. Brown. "Where shall we begin, Alex?"

"Begin with Old Tail, Tale," said Alex, "because she's youngest, and then go up by ages."

Mrs. Brown handed Helga one of the packages and while everyone watched she opened it. In it was a pink parasol, as pink as the wild roses that grew by the roadside; and it had a white border with little pink roses on it. Nobody there had ever seen such a beautiful parasol.

"Mamma, Mamma!" said Helga when she could speak. "Is it really mine?"

One by one the other girls opened their packages, and every parasol was as beautiful as the one before it.

"I didn't even know there were so many beautiful parasols in the whole world!" said Elsa, looking at her lovely light green one with its border of white and yellow daisies. Sigrid's had a white background with blue forget-me-nots on it; and Wanda's was white with a bunch of violets decorating one side of it.

"I tried to get one with yellow roses for you, Nancy," said Mrs. Brown, "but there weren't any in any of the stores."

Nancy was perfectly satisfied with hers. It was all yellow and the edge was scalloped; and the scallops looked like the petals of a rose.

"When you carry it where the sun is shining through it," said Grandma, "it will be like being right in the center of a yellow rose."

"This is a NINE-MILLION-times-nicer name day," said Sigrid.

The little girls were so surprised by Mrs. Brown's wonderful presents that they could hardly say thank you; but all the grownups told her over and over again how much they appreciated her thoughtfulness.

"But think of what you have all done for Alex," she said, looking at his happy face.

It was now after four o'clock.

"We must be getting back to the farmhouse," said Grandpa. "Uncle Sven will want to do the milking while Alex can watch him. But first I have something I'd like to say to you all." He smiled his gentle, sweet smile at the people sitting around him and slowly drew from his pocket—the Almanac.

He turned it over in his hands two or three times without saying anything, while they all waited. Then he began:

"I have been thinking a good deal, as we all have, about a name day for Nancy; but I was no better than any of the rest of you—and not so good as Wanda—at finding a way to get one for her. Then, a few nights ago, I picked up the Almanac and I noticed something I had never noticed before."

He paused a moment. There was something in the way he spoke that made everyone feel that he was going to say something important. He went on:

"I noticed that there is one day that has no name beside it. I do not know why I never saw this before except that there is so much other printing beside the dates that the fact that there is no name doesn't show much. And I think when you children were hunting in the Almanac you looked only at *names* and did not realize that you were beginning with January 2. There is no name for January 1."

The little girls crowded around him to look.

"I never noticed that either," said Uncle Sven. "I wonder why that is so?"

"I have to admit that I don't know," said Grandpa.

"Maybe there weren't enough Swedish names to go for all the days," said Elsa.

"I know what," said Sigrid. "Maybe the people that made the Almanac knew that all Swedish people might have some friend who wasn't Swedish and might want to give her a name day!"

"Well," said Grandpa, "whatever the reason, it seems to me that, as Sigrid says, we could give a dear friend a name day. I should like all of you people here to think carefully and tell me how you feel it would be if we should put Nancy's name at January 1 in our Swedish Almanac. If you all think it would be a good idea, that is what I shall do. And Sven, will you then write her name in yours, and John, will you write it in yours? Not only this year, but every year as soon as your new Almanac comes?"

"That I will gladly do," said Uncle Sven.

"And so will I," said Uncle John.

"And," said Elsa, "when we grow up and have Almanacs of our own, we'll always write Nancy's name in and we'll tell our children and grandchildren to do the same, and the name of Nancy will appear on January 1 in every Almanac in the houses of Benson and Carlson forever!"

"I can see," said Grandpa, "that some of you agree. Do you all?"

And it was plain that all the Bensons and the Carlsons did.

Nancy stood looking at Grandpa. He turned now and smiled directly at her.

"And you, Nancy, what do you think?" he asked.

"Never mind if there aren't any flowers on January 1, Nancy," said Elsa. "We'll still have Christmas greens, and we could make you a crown with greens and lighted candles like a Saint Lucia crown."

Now whether Nancy would have been satisfied with this kind of name day if the plan had been suggested to her earlier, nobody—not even she herself—would ever know. But while Elsa was speaking, Nancy suddenly saw a name day as glowing and golden with lighted candles as this one was with yellow buttercups and daisies. Candles all over the house—in the windows, on the tree, on the party table, even in her crown. A lovely golden name day all her own!

"I think I would like it, Grandpa," she said.

"Could you write her name with that funny blue indelible pencil that nobody can ever erase?" asked Sigrid.

"That is the very pencil I brought to write it with," said Grandpa. "And when my new Almanac comes for next year, I will write Nancy in that, and Nancy shall have this old one as a souvenir of this day." He took out his pencil.

"This is a solemn moment," said Elsa. "We should all sing something."

"What shall we sing, Nancy?" said Uncle John.

"You say, Elsa," said Nancy.

" *'Tryggare Kan Ingen Vara,'* " said Elsa immediately and turned to Mrs. Brown and Alex to explain. "That is one of our favorites. It's about how safe God's little children are because He takes care of them all—safer than the stars in the heavens, safer than the little birds in their cozy nests. I think we should sing it now because this shows things come out all right in the end. Nancy really has a name day all her own."

And so they began to sing, and Grandpa took the Almanac and settling it on his knee with the book open at January, he wrote opposite the first —carefully and clearly:

Nancy